THE MAD REAPER

JASON JAMES KING

Immortal Works LLC
1527 Glenrose Drive
Salt Lake City, Utah 84104
Tel: (385) 202-0116

Cover Art by Megan King

ISBN: 978-1-953491-75-6
AISN: B0CD3PSRD1

For Debbie,
You've always been my rock.
I love you, Ma.

PROLOGUE

CHARLES BENSON

DETECTIVE CHARLES "CHUCK" Benson hated staying in motels. It wasn't the over-shampooed carpet, or the moldy shower curtains he always seemed to find in the bathrooms. It wasn't even the bedbug roulette he played each time he laid his black ass down on a mattress soiled by every fluid the human body could produce. No, the reason Chuck hated motels was each time he checked into one, his wife, Irene, accused him of not checking in alone.

Never mind that Chuck had been wholeheartedly faithful to Irene since their wedding day fifteen years ago. Never mind that he never called the office secretary by her first name or even so much as mentioned to her when she looked nice–and she *always* looked nice. Never mind that he was a devout Baptist who went to church, read his Bible, and prayed to Jesus every morning and every night. None of those things mattered to Irene if Chuck decided to stay the night at a motel; he might as well have been partying with Hugh Hefner and a dozen Playboy Bunnies as far as she was concerned.

That's why he was driving this lonely forest road at two AM. He'd traveled ninety miles across the county line to interview a woman who'd found a corpse stuffed into her chicken coop. He'd thought it might be connected to a case he was working, but it turned out the man wasn't so much "stuffed" as he was "stuck," and the chickens had done the rest.

I'm never going to KFC again!

Well, it'd taken all day to determine the death wasn't a homicide. Just the accidental death of a cold, homeless man looking for shelter perpetrated by angry chickens. He tried not to chuckle, but when you were in this line of work, death was funny. It had to be, or you'd go insane.

Chuck yawned. With thick forest on either side of him it was like he was driving through an endless tunnel. Folks didn't realize how dark the night could get when there were no streetlights or buildings or houses for miles.

He reached for his coffee, took a sip, and nearly spit it out. It'd already gone cold, but he forced himself to swallow. If he was going to survive the remaining two-hour drive, he needed the caffeine.

"Should've got a Coke," he muttered.

As the night wore on, and his eyes drooped, Chuck started thinking a motel might've been worth the domestic trouble. Yeah, he would've caught all kinds of hell, but better in the doghouse than the graveyard, right?

He was starting to wonder if Irene would prefer him in the ground. Dark thoughts like that led him to dark places, and more than once he found himself flirting with the idea of leaving the garage door closed after starting up his car. But that wasn't who Chuck Benson was. He couldn't do that to his Lord and Savior, or his mama.

But Irene really was trying him these days. Her demands were becoming increasingly unreasonable. They were working on their issues with their minister, but Chuck wasn't seeing any progress. The Bible said divorce was wrong, but was he really supposed to live out his life putting up with her abuse? Not that she hit him, but she was convinced he couldn't do anything right, and often said things that hurt worse than any physical pain.

Irene's most vicious attack, the one that sent Chuck's mind to dark places, was her accusation that it was his fault they couldn't have children. That somehow, Chuck's time in the army had made him sterile. It was true they hadn't been able to conceive, but the doctors all agreed that, while they didn't know what the cause of their infertility was, it was definitely not a problem with his equipment. Of course, Irene wouldn't listen to anyone when she thought she was right. Be it Chuck, the doctor, their minister, or probably even The Almighty Himself if He—

Chuck's headlights reflected on something in the road directly in his path, and whether by reflexes or over-caffeinated nerves or both, Chuck swerved into the other lane and slammed on his brakes. The car fishtailed briefly before he came to a crooked stop across both lanes. He glanced in the rearview mirror half expecting to find nothing and finally earn a ghost story he could tell his buddies, but the figure he'd caught in his sight remained.

"What the hell?"

Chuck slowly pulled his car forward and parked it as far to the right as he could, the passenger side tires resting on the dirt almost to the tree line. He flicked on the hazards, left the engine running and the lights on, and opened his door.

Resting his right hand on the grip of his Glock, he held his radio in the other hand and slowly made his way around the back of his car. He thought about opening the trunk to retrieve his flashlight, but that might startle the child.

Chuck clicked on his radio. "Benson 10-39?"

No response.

He made another attempt and was met again with static.

"Shit," he hissed.

The child walked into the radiance of the car's lights. It was a boy, probably around ten-years-old, maybe eleven—lean but not skinny. He had mud all over his face and wore a red T-shirt, maybe tie-dyed? It was hard to tell in the blinking red of the hazard lights.

"Hey, buddy," Chuck said, trying to sound non-threatening. He'd never been good with kids. "It's ok, I'm a policeman." He motioned at the shield on his belt.

The boy stopped but didn't look up at him.

"What're you doing out here in the middle of the night? Where are your parents?"

The boy didn't answer.

"You cold?"

Chuck slowly reached to open his trunk, and when it sprang open, he half expected the boy to jump, but he stood frozen as though he'd been sleepwalking.

Without turning his back to the boy, Chuck found his emergency bag and fished out a blanket and a flashlight. He clicked the flashlight on and shined it on the boy.

"Oh shit!"

It wasn't mud on the boy's face, nor was his T-shirt red. He was covered from head to toe in blood. His bare feet left bloody prints on the pavement behind him.

The boy looked up at Chuck, a silent plea in his blue eyes. A tear trailed a runnel through the dry blood on his face, soon followed by more, and then, like a dam bursting, the boy fell to his knees and sobbed. Chuck ran to him, put the blanket around the boy's shoulders, and sat with him on the ground.

"Hey, buddy, it's going to be ok, I promise." After making sure the blood covering the boy didn't belong to him, Chuck rubbed his back like his mama used to do for him when he was upset.

The boy nestled his head in Chuck's chest and sobbed for five straight minutes until he fell asleep. At first Chuck was surprised that the kid could fall asleep with a total stranger, in the middle of the night, on a deserted road, but it made sense.

He's exhausted from whatever hell he's just escaped.

Chuck scooped up the boy and carried him to his car where he awkwardly opened the rear driver's side door and laid the sleeping boy in the back seat. He closed the trunk before getting in the car and pulling back onto the road. He wouldn't be going home tonight, and the only thing that upset Irene more than his staying in a motel, was when Chuck's job kept him out all night.

Well, if she didn't like it, to hell with her. He was done trying to placate her. If Irene was going to raise hell over him staying out to rescue a little boy covered in blood, she wasn't the Christian woman he'd married fifteen years ago.

Perhaps she'd never really been that woman.

Chuck glanced into the back seat. The boy was still sleeping, but not peacefully. His eyes darted back and forth behind his eyelids, and his body jerked as he whimpered at whatever horrors lurked in his dreams.

"You're safe now, Buddy."

That apparently soothed the boy, and he quieted.

"No more nightmares," Chuck whispered.

From the time I was a young man I heard the call of God to the Priesthood. While most men my age chased girls and engaged in sports, I devoted myself to the study of God's holy word. I wanted to help people. That desire burned within me so hot that it became a kind of obsession. I thought that was good, but the devil is clever. If he can't tempt man with evil, he will seek to corrupt the holy until it becomes disfigured. I am disfigured. He took my desire to help people and twisted it.

JOURNAL OF FATHER KEVIN ALLEN DRAKES

CHAPTER
ONE

JORDAN GRIFFIN, tall with short, dirty-blond hair parted on the side, wearing a button-down shirt and slacks, was the very image of what the bureau expected their agents to look like. He knew that, and found pride in it, even if it did draw the ridicule of some of his fellows. Their sarcasm and mostly harmless jabs didn't bother Jordan, not really. He was a true believer in the agency and what they stood for—justice. He was not just an agent of the bureau, but an agent of justice. And after a long fight, today justice would prevail.

Jordan nodded to the agents flanking the office door. They were dressed in full tactical gear and bore fully automatic assault rifles, a ridiculous sight considering the room they were guarding was the field office's onsite gym. But it was the only room in the building without windows, perfect for tonight's purpose. Jordan glanced at his watch.

Not tonight–this morning.

It was nearing 3AM, an ungodly hour for anyone to be up. That was the hope anyway.

"Savage, Erickson." Jordan greeted the agents.

"Agent Griffin," Erickson, standing on the right side of the door, said with a nod.

"Here." Jordan extended two Styrofoam cups, one in each hand.

Steam from their contents wafted up as Erickson took one, followed by Savage.

Savage smiled. "Bless you, Griffin."

"It's not charity. It's fuel. I need you two awake and alert."

Erickson chuckled before taking a sip of his coffee.

"This shit-eater better be worth it," Savage said. "When my five-year-old found out her daddy had to miss her birthday party, she folded her arms, stuck her chin in the air, and marched straight to her room. Gonna have to buy her a pony just to get her to talk to me again."

"Sounds just like her mama." Erickson smirked. "Tell Griffin what it cost you when you missed your anniversary last year."

"A diamond bracelet." Savage took another sip.

Erickson whistled. "That's why I have a cat."

"Trust me, it'll be worth it." Jordan reached into the pocket of his charcoal-colored slacks and fished out a keycard.

Erickson and Savage took the cue and stepped away from the door. Jordan raised his keycard to the reader, causing the light on the plastic box to flash green. He turned the handle down and pushed open the door.

A balding man sat on the corner of one of the room's treadmills. He pushed his horn-rimmed glasses up the bridge of his nose. The collar of his white button-down shirt hung loosely around his skinny neck, reminding Jordan of a vulture.

Perfect comparison.

Next to the treadmill was an army cot where the man had tossed his rumpled suit jacket. He started as Jordan entered the room, and then ran a hand over his balding head. "Couldn't knock first?"

Jordan let the door shut behind him and glanced at the cot. "Can't sleep, Casey?"

"Would you be able to sleep knowing that Edward Alexander wanted *you* dead?"

"He probably does want me dead." Jordan leaned down and picked up a large, beige duffle bag from beside the door.

Casey laughed. "He probably doesn't even know your name, Agent Griffin."

Jordan ground his teeth. For some reason, that stung.

"It's time." Jordan walked over to Casey and dropped the duffle bag at his feet. "Put these on."

Casey unzipped the duffle, fished in it, and pulled out a SWAT helmet.

"There's also a vest inside." Jordan turned and walked back toward the door.

"It won't help me," Casey called.

Jordan stopped in front of the door, hand on the handle. "We'll protect you, Pierce."

Casey coughed out a hysterical sob. "I was screwed the second you arrested me."

"We won't let Alexander kill you, Pierce."

"Kill me?" Casey laughed. "I wish that were it. No, he's going to make an example out of me. And then, when it's all over, he'll let his guard dogs have me. And I'm not talking about canines. I mean his enforcers. Psychopaths like Dawson and Reese."

Victor Reese.

Jordan clenched his jaw. Reese was head of Alexander's personal cadre of enforcers—the soldiers that did his dirty work. Jordan had met Victor Reese only once but knew so much about him he felt like he personally knew the man.

Reese was about Jordan's age–thirty-two—and athletic, with features most women would consider handsome, and was a suspect in over twelve murders. Though he most certainly had committed more. Alexander may have been the architect of those murders, but Reese was the killer. Cold and as vicious as he was ruthless, Jordan didn't blame Pierce for being frightened of him.

"If you're so afraid, why'd you talk to us? Why not just go to prison?"

"For Dylan. I'm doing this for him."

It sounded to Jordan like Pierce wasn't speaking to *him* but reminding himself.

"Will he be safe, Agent Griffin?"

Jordan stared at the criminal, and it was like he was seeing him for the first time. Did Pierce view this as a sacrifice? Was his turning state's witness a distraction just so the FBI could get his family out of the city and into witness protection?

"Dylan and your wife safely made it to—"

"Don't tell me!" Pierce snapped. "I can't know where you sent them. He can't find out!"

"Relax, Casey. You keep up your end of the deal, and you'll be joining them before you know it. The bureau got you a job teaching high school math. I think the fact that you'll be spending your days in classes with surly, hormonal teens should spook you more than this trip to DC."

Pierce barked out a laugh, but it was entirely devoid of humor.

He really believes he's going to die tonight.

"Put on the gear. It's almost time to go."

Jordan left the gym, but not before catching a soft "Dylan," from Pierce.

"Make sure he's ready in ten," Jordan ordered Savage and Erickson, not giving them time to respond before striding down the hall.

The sincerity of Pierce's words had shaken Jordan's confidence. He'd been sure the weaselly accountant had taken the immunity deal in the interest of saving his own skin. But the man Jordan just spoke to sounded like a man on his way to the gallows, striving to find meaning in his death.

Jordan reached into his right pants pocket where he found a small coin. It was a challenge coin he'd received from a four-star general in Iraq from his time in the service as an Army Ranger—bronze and emblazoned with a shield, lightning bolt, and the phrase *Rangers Lead the Way*. He'd kept it in his pocket nearly every day since, as a sort of a totem. He wasn't superstitious, but he liked to think it brought him good luck, and tonight he'd need all the luck he could get.

Jordan bypassed the elevators and took the stairs four flights down to the parking garage where he was greeted by a dozen agents milling about four black SUVs. Several of the agents were dressed in tactical gear like Savage and Erickson.

He was stopped by a middle-aged, overweight man with a thinning hair line. His rumpled suit had seen better days. "You're late, Griffin," growled Assistant Special Agent in Charge Adam Seigers.

And you're an asshole.

"I was prepping Mr. Pierce."

ASAC Seigers just grunted. The man was one of the most thoroughly unpleasant people Jordan had worked with in his career at the FBI, someone who hated field work. Jordan suspected Seigers once had designs on higher positions but failed to successfully navigate the bureaucracy and so was now just running out the clock to get his pension. It made him a joy to work with.

A short, brown-skinned man stood with a group of the SWAT agents, holding a large tablet to which they were gathered round. When he saw Jordan he waved him over.

"I better go," he said to Seigers, leaving before he could reply.

As Jordan approached, the man finished up his presentation with an "Everyone got that?" The SWAT agents nodded and then dispersed.

"Updates?" Jordan asked.

"And a good morning to you too, Jordan!" The short man tapped the screen of his tablet, causing it to zoom in on a map of city streets.

Jordan chuckled. "Sorry, Miguel. It's just too early for me."

"Liar," Miguel snapped. "I know for a fact you're up every day at 0400 to go jogging."

Jordan nodded. "Once a soldier, always a soldier."

Miguel scoffed. "Nah, you're just weird. When I got out of the service I went right back to sleeping in."

"Until you had kids."

Miguel sighed. "Until I had kids."

"Making changes?" Jordan took the tablet from him.

Miguel shook his head. "Just adding another rally point in case we have to abort."

"Looks good." Jordan handed it back to him. "But I want to make one more change."

Miguel swiped on the tablet, shrinking the map. "Yeah?"

"I want to ride with you and Pierce."

Miguel's head snapped up. "Why?"

"That a problem?"

"No, I just feel better having you bring up the rear." Miguel shrugged. "That's all."

Jordan glanced over his shoulder at the door to the stairs leading back up into the office building. "Erickson and Savage can bring up the rear."

"Why change things up?"

Jordan turned back to his friend. "Change keeps the enemy off-balance."

"You've been talking to Pierce."

"He's really convinced Alexander can get to him." Jordan shot a glance at the set of elevator doors that serviced the parking garage.

Miguel shook his head. "We have a convoy of unmarked vehicles manned by six agents with SWAT support and LSPD squad cars stationed all along our route to a private airfield. No one's getting to Pierce!"

"Still, I'd feel better riding with you."

Miguel sharply jabbed the tablet's screen. "You're a real pain in my ass, you know that?"

Jordan scoffed. "See? There is something you and Kate can agree on."

Miguel cocked an eyebrow. "Another newlywed spat?"

"We're not newlyweds—we've been married almost three years."

Miguel scoffed. "My twelve against your three says you're still newlyweds."

"That's fair."

"You know the bureau has support groups for couples and their spouses, right?"

"A bunch of disgruntled agents' wives meeting to complain about their husbands? Sounds like a divorce lawyer's wet dream."

Miguel lowered the tablet. "This why you wanna ride with me? To bitch about your problems? Because if it is, then…"

Jordan shook his head. "No, I…"

Before he could continue, the elevator chimed and its doors opened. Savage stepped out followed by Erickson who was towing Pierce by the elbow. The scrawny accountant was wearing the SWAT helmet and bullet-proof vest Jordan had given him. He'd look comical if it wasn't for the forlorn expression on his face.

Their eyes met, and Jordan held Pierce's gaze until the man couldn't handle it and looked away.

"Come on, Jordan. Just leave Pierce to me, and when this is all over I'll buy you breakfast." Miguel playfully swatted Jordan's bicep with his tablet. "We can go to that place that makes those chocolate chip pancakes."

Jordan looked down at Miguel. "You mean the place managed by that blonde who always leaves her top button undone?"

Miguel grinned. "I sure do love her pancakes."

"Sorry, partner." Jordan put his hand on Miguel's shoulder. "I'm riding with you."

They made the riding assignment changes quickly, and in a few short minutes four black SUVs pulled out of the parking garage and onto the virtually deserted city streets. As planned, the convoy made random, unexpected turns and took a circuitous route to the highway, just in case they were being tailed. Aside from making Pierce car-sick, they had no trouble. Jordan suspected Miguel was driving a little more erratic than necessary for that exact purpose. Normally Jordan would find that funny, but after talking with Pierce, his feelings for the man had started to change, and he found himself pitying him.

Aside from the agent in SWAT gear–Simmons was her name—sitting next to Pierce in the backseat trying to make small talk, the cab of the SUV was silent. Which was a bit odd, usually Miguel would be talking Jordan's ear off by now.

"You ok there, partner?" Jordan asked.

Miguel nodded.

"Hey, if I pissed you off changing up your plan—"

"Not in front of the cargo," Miguel snapped.

Jordan glanced back at Pierce. "All right."

More awkward silence followed.

"How about some music?" Jordan shared a look with Simmons. "What's your pleasure, Casey?"

"Nineties alternative," Pierce muttered.

"Sounds good."

He found a nineties alternative station on internet radio and the first song served up was "Insanity" by Oingo Boingo. It wasn't exactly a soothing song, but Pierce didn't object, so Jordan let the music play while the four passengers sat in contemplative silence. Jordan stared out the window, watching the towering streetlamps rhythmically pass as they sped down a sparsely occupied highway.

His thoughts drifted back to his wife, Kate. They'd had a particularly nasty fight before he left the night prior. Unlike other agents, their fighting wasn't about the tumultuous, unpredictable life of an FBI agent. Kate was an emergency room nurse and was accustomed to long, aberrant working hours, which made her well suited to be the wife of a special agent. No, Kate found the bottle of vodka Jordan had hidden in his tool-box–a mostly empty bottle.

He'd done well over the last eight months, only slipping once at a wedding reception for Kate's brother. Now it looked like Jordan would be going back to weekly meetings, and he and Kate would be seeing a counselor.

"Why?" she'd asked. And Jordan couldn't give her an answer. "Don't I make you happy?"

Kate *did* make him happy, ridiculously happy. But his drinking wasn't about happiness, it never had been. It was about trying to forget.

He was ten years old again, standing in a dirty kitchen holding a bloody butcher's knife.

The high-pitched whine of a motorcycle snapped Jordan out of his reverie. He checked the rearview mirror. A man in a gray trench coat, riding a bullet bike, weaved in front of their companion SUV just behind them.

"Who does this asshole think he is?" Simmons asked as she stared out the rear window.

Jordan lifted his radio and clicked it on. "Savage, what's the deal with the biker?"

The radio crackled and Savage responded, "He was riding our bumper for a minute. Guess we're too slow for him."

The trench coat biker accelerated, weaved into the lane at their right, and then cut directly in front of the SUV Miguel was piloting.

"No plate," Simmons observed.

Jordan clicked his radio. "Savage, alert highway patrol that..." he trailed off.

The trench coat biker sped forward until he was mere inches behind the SUV in front of them.

"Agent Griffin?" Savage's voice called over the radio.

The trench coat biker reached into his coat, pulled out a brick-shaped object, and slapped it on the SUV's bumper, where it stuck. Then he veered right and crossed four lanes, barely avoiding a collision as several cars pelted him with angry honks. The trench coat biker rode into the exit lane and sped down an off-ramp. Jordan glanced back at the object stuck to the SUV in front of them. A single glowing red dot blinked back at him.

"Shit!" Jordan swore.

The world turned to fire.

An explosion from behind them rocked the SUV, shattering its rear window. Simmons shrieked, and Pierce screamed. Before they could recover, another explosion erupted from the SUV in front of them. Miguel cranked the steering wheel hard to the right just in time for them to circumvent the flaming wreckage, and he started to slow as they crossed into the neighboring lanes.

"Don't stop!" Jordan shouted.

Miguel, blood leaking down his face, nodded and accelerated.

"She's hurt!" Pierce shouted from the backseat.

Jordan turned to find Agent Simmons slumped over, her helmet missing, and blood gushing where a piece of shrapnel protruded from her neck.

Jordan released his seatbelt and climbed half-way into a backseat littered with broken glass and gnarled pieces of metal. He grabbed Pierce's wrist, directing his hand to Simmons' wound.

"Keep pressure there!"

"Oh shit," Pierce breathed as his hand touched Simmons' bloody neck.

A chorus of speeding motorcycles drew Jordan's attention back to the road. He lowered himself back into the passenger seat and drew his Glock. Two bikers sped up along the SUV's right side. The bikers leveled their submachine guns and sprayed the SUV with bullets, leaving small, round craters in the vehicle's bullet-proof side windows.

"Don't let them get behind us!" Jordan shouted at Miguel.

But it was too late.

One of the bikers had noticed the missing rear window, slowed, and crossed into their lane so he was closing in on their bumper. His companion quickly followed. Jordan turned in his seat, aimed his Glock, and squeezed off six rounds. The last two shots took the foremost biker in the chest, and he fell sideways, his bike throwing up sparks as it skidded under the wheels of his companion, causing him to wreck.

"We need to get to a rally point," Jordan shouted.

"I'm trying!" Miguel shouted back.

The whine of accelerating bike engines multiplied until a chorus of high-pitched buzzing signaled their assailants' reinforcements had arrived. Sure enough, four more bikers appeared behind them, closing the distance as they roared forward.

"Slide over!" Jordan barked at Pierce.

Pierce complied by sliding over to Simmons, all the while keeping his hand awkwardly over her gushing wound. Jordan holstered his service weapon, climbed into the back seat, and reached for Simmons' assault rifle lying on the floor. He knelt on the SUV's back bench and hoisted the rifle to his shoulder, aiming it out the massive hole where moments before a rear window had been.

Two bikers raced forward, pulled pistols, and aimed. Jordan sprayed them with automatic fire, and they went down before they could squeeze off a single shot. The two remaining bikers raced up beside the SUV, one on the right and one in the emergency lane on the left. Pierce screamed and hunched over Simmons as bullets thudded against the armored cab.

"Get us off the freeway, Miguel!" Jordan shouted.

"Next exit isn't for another two miles!"

"Then we make our own exit!" Jordan dropped the assault rifle, turned, and climbed halfway into the front over the center console.

He reached over Miguel's shoulder and cranked the wheel to the right. The SUV lurched into the travel lane, plowing over the biker on that side, then it crossed three lanes and broke through an aluminum guard rail. Jordan's head repeatedly slammed into the roof as they bounced down a grassy hill. He gripped the front passenger seat but was thrown forward, his forehead striking the dashboard. The SUV landed, and Jordan found himself in the front passenger side of the SUV, his back against the dash, and his feet still resting on the center console. He quickly righted himself and glanced around. They'd landed on a frontage road that ran parallel to the highway.

Miguel slammed on the brakes. "¡Que demonios!"

"Don't stop!" Jordan shouted back. "Get us to that rally point!"

Miguel continued muttering to himself in Spanish but did as Jordan ordered.

They raced down the frontage road, the wail of sirens echoing in the distance. Jordan

reached into the back seat, pushed Pierce's hand away, and checked Simmons' neck for a pulse.

Nothing.

"Damn it!" He leaned back in the seat. He wanted to scream and smash out a window, not that it would take much. The glass was no longer transparent, but white and threaded through with spiderweb-like cracks.

Miguel said nothing as they took a circuitous route through the connecting streets of an industrial area. Finally, they pulled into the parking lot of an old textiles factory, one long abandoned as indicated by the boarded-up windows and the cracked and crumbling asphalt.

There was a dark sedan waiting for them. Jordan didn't recognize the car and opened his mouth to ask Miguel who they were meeting when a man in a trench coat, riding a bullet bike, sped into the parking lot. It was the same man who'd blown up the motorcade.

Jordan turned to Miguel just as his partner raised his Glock, not at the biker, but at him. He lunged at Miguel, forcing his hand down and away from his head. A shot rang out, and Pierce screamed. A blow to Jordan's side forced the breath out of him, and his ears rang. The gut punch started to sting and burn, followed by hot liquid running down his side. He gasped for air and fell back against the passenger door. His eyes met Miguel's, and Jordan found anger in his partner's stare.

"You stubborn son of a bitch! Why'd you have to insist on riding with me?" Miguel's voice was strained, almost hysterical. He crossed himself and muttered, "*Dios Perdoname!*"

"Sandoval!" a bass voice called.

Miguel opened his door and stepped out. A burly Black man dressed in a suit emerged from the sedan, the tightfitting T-shirt beneath the suit jacket revealing his sculpted, muscular physique. Jordan frowned. David Sadler, one of Alexander's lead enforcers.

No…Miguel.

The *chief* of Alexander's cadre of enforcers, Victor Reese, emerged from the passenger side of the sedan, running a hand through his wavy black hair as he flashed his movie star smile in Jordan's direction.

Jordan glanced at the trench coat clad man on the bullet bike. He removed his helmet and, where Reese was groomed and handsome, this man had shaggy hair, a patchy tangled beard, and looked homeless. But his dead-eyed stare was unmistakable. It was Christian Dawson, Reese's pet psychopath.

"What the hell was that!" Miguel threw up his arms. "You didn't tell me you were going to blow up the whole damned motorcade!"

"Did you get Pierce?" Reese asked, ignoring Miguel's tirade.

Miguel waved a hand at the SUV. "Did you get my pay?"

Reese walked over to it. "One million, as promised, already transferred to your offshore account." He peeked in through the open driver's door. "Hello, Casey."

Pierce responded with a whimper.

Then Reese glanced at Jordan. "Agent Griffin?" His gaze fell to Jordan's bloody shirt, and he frowned. "You said Agent Griffin would be bringing up the rear of the motorcade."

"Not my fault!" Miguel shouted. "And why the hell were your men shooting at us?"

Reese straightened. "Had to make it look real."

"Did you have to make it look *that* real?" Miguel brushed glass out of his hair. "Thanks to you we have to put down my partner! And you're gonna have to shoot me too." Miguel motioned to his leg.

Reese turned to face him, and then unceremoniously shot him in the head. Jordan flinched and watched helplessly as his partner crumpled to the ground.

"David," Reese called.

Sadler walked over, opened the SUV's rear driver's side door, and extricated Pierce. The skinny man tried to resist, but his strength was nothing compared to that of the muscular Sadler. He babbled and pled as he was towed away and forced into the backset of Reese's sedan.

Reese looked back at Jordan. "I'm sincerely sorry, Agent Griffin."

Jordan closed his eyes, ready for the bullet, but instead of a gunshot, he heard ringing. Jordan opened his eyes and found Reese on his phone.

"9-1-1 what's your emergency?" came the distant voice of a woman.

"There are three FBI agents down at three-sixty-five Syracuse Way. Please send help fast." Reese lowered the phone and punched the screen with his index finger to end the call. "Help is coming, Agent Griffin."

"Why?" Jordan wheezed.

Reese locked eyes with him and smiled. "Get well soon, agent." He walked away and climbed into his waiting car.

Jordan watched the sedan pull out of the parking lot, followed by Dawson on his bullet bike. He tried to move, but the pain and a frightening weakness prevented him from doing more than adjusting in his blood-soaked seat. He fought the darkness fuzzing the edges of his vision, but it was too much for him. The last thing Jordan heard was sirens.

I truly seek to love all of God's children, sinners most of all. But some sinners, the ones that hurt the innocent, I have not found much love in my heart for them. My mercy especially falters with those who victimize children. Instead of charity, I feel a sense of indignation. I don't want them to cry and confess. I want them to suffer.

JOURNAL OF FATHER KEVIN ALLEN DRAKES

CHAPTER
TWO

VICTOR REESE LISTENED to the chatter of the police scanner broadcasting to his earpiece. First responders had found Griffin, and they were transporting him to a hospital. He unclenched his teeth. From what the EMTs were saying, Griffin was stable.

What was that imbecile Sandoval thinking?

Well, the man wasn't a genius, that was certain. Victor often found that law enforcement officers who would accept bribes weren't all that bright.

"R-Reese," Pierce stammered. "Where are you taking me?"

Victor glanced into the back seat. Pierce's collar was open, his tie missing, and he had sweat through his shirt. "Wouldn't want to spoil the surprise."

"Victor."

Victor looked at the man driving the sedan—David Sadler.

"The money promised to Sandoval?"

Victor glanced at his phone. "You want it? It's yours."

"No," David replied. "Can we make sure it reaches Agent Sandoval's widow?"

Victor smiled. David—his closest and oldest friend—though criminal, soldier, and murderer, was a man of indisputable honor. It was an odd contradiction, and one of the things Victor loved about him. It also made it difficult to get things done sometimes. David's moral compunctions made him ill-suited to some of their more repugnant assignments. Anytime the harming or killing of women and children was necessary, David couldn't be relied on. That's why Victor had Dawson. Victor glanced in the rearview mirror and found Dawson following closely on his bullet bike.

Where David was difficult to motivate to violence, Dawson was difficult to restrain. The psychopath had an unholy enthusiasm when it came to dealing out brutality and death. Victor suspected that if Dawson wasn't in his employ, the man would be the topic of presentation for countless profilers and investigative journalists.

You would've liked him, Uncle Simon.

Victor opened an app on his phone and re-routed the money transfer. "The FBI will want to seize it, so we'll have to get creative on how we deliver it, but I'll make sure it gets to her."

"Thank you," David said.

Victor glanced into the backseat again. Pierce was pale and trembling, and by the smell of it, had wet himself.

"Come on, Casey! Show some grace under pressure."

Pierce squeezed his eyes shut and whimpered.

Twenty minutes of driving took them back into the city proper where they descended a ramp into an underground parking garage beneath a glass high-rise. Sadler drove the sedan down three levels and parked near a set of elevators. Dawson pulled his bullet bike into the stall next to them. Victor emerged from the car, greeted by a group of six of his men. Sadler pulled Pierce from the backseat and controlled him by bunching up the back of the man's collar.

They took the elevator to the penthouse, the stainless steel doors opening to reveal a posh lounge full of finely dressed men accompanied by beautiful, scandalously dressed women who were certainly not their wives or girlfriends. Large screens covered one wall and set opposite, were leather recliners to facilitate comfortable viewing. The screens showed an arena filled with spectators, at the center of which was an MMA cage with two muscular, shirtless men inside, beating on each other to the delight of the crowd.

A server approached with a tray of drinks. Victor waved them away, but before the server could retreat, Dawson took two flutes of champagne, pouring both into his mouth at the same time, causing the bubbly liquid to dribble into his patchy beard and onto his trench coat.

Victor smiled and led his entourage through a crowd of party guests to a finely dressed, middle-aged man taking a drag on a cigar. He sat in a high-backed chair set on a dais that raised him higher than the other chairs, allowing him an unobstructed view of the screens. It reminded Victor of a throne, which was appropriate, because the man was none other than Edward Alexander–ruler of Lake Side City's underworld. He was a boss of bosses, and therefore a modern-day urban emperor.

Pierce squeaked when he caught sight of Alexander and pulled against David's grip, but it was futile. The traitor could not escape the judgment that was coming for him.

"Victor!" Alexander stood and descended three steps.

Victor waved at Pierce. "Casey Pierce, as ordered."

Edward Alexander stepped past Victor and stared down at Pierce. He flashed a cruel grin and then extinguished his cigar on the cowering man's cheek. Pierce choked out a scream, and David released his arm so he could collapse to his knees. He pressed a hand to his burnt cheek and sobbed.

"Pathetic," Alexander spat.

"Please," Pierce pled. "I'm sorry, Mr. Alexander."

"It's too late for that, I'm afraid."

Pierce melted into a sniveling heap.

"You betrayed me, Pierce. I don't care what your motive was. You know the rules of our company. You know the penalty."

Reese glanced at the man to his side. "Dawson."

Dawson smiled and took a step toward Pierce.

Alexander raised a hand to forestall him. "I have something else in mind."

Pierce looked up; his tear-stained face completely white.

Alexander stepped away and addressed the room. "This pathetic nobody turned on us to save his own worthless skin."

The party guests jeered, and someone threw a cocktail shrimp at Pierce. He flinched as it glanced off his shoulder. Alexander turned to stare at the dozens of screens displaying the cage match. One of the large, muscular men had his opponent in a headlock. After a moment's struggle, he jerked his arms, twisting his opponent's head to the side, snapping his neck. The spectators watching from outside the cage shook the chain-link fence that separated them from the arena and roared with delight.

Alexander turned from the screens and smiled down at Pierce. "We're going to let Mr. Pierce fight for his life in the Lethal Games!"

The room exploded into laughter. Victor caught a frown from David. His friend obviously disapproved of turning Pierce's execution into entertainment for Alexander's rich sycophants. Truth be told, Victor didn't like it either. But that was Alexander. The man was sometimes more showman than crime boss. If it were up to Victor, he would just put a bullet in Pierce's head and be done with it. But he understood what Alexander was doing. He wasn't only putting on a show for his supporters, he was sending a message.

"If Mr. Pierce kills his opponent, he will win back his life and walk out of here a free man!"

"I'm not a fighter!" Pierce protested, but Alexander ignored him.

"And to make things especially interesting, I will choose a past champion to face Mr. Pierce in the ring!" Alexander walked over to David, grabbed his hand, and raised his arm up. "David Sadler!"

David's eyes widened as he shot a silent plea to Victor.

"Mr. Alexander," David started, "I can't."

Alexander dropped his hand and patted David on the back. "Don't be modest, Mr. Sadler! I know it's been a few years, but you're still as fierce as ever." Alexander faced his guests, smiled, and traced his fingers over David's muscled chest. "And as fit as ever."

That elicited a catcall from one of the men in the room and everyone laughed.

David moved to Victor and leaned in close to whisper, "Victor, don't make me do this."

"You know I can't stop it," Victor whispered back.

Alexander stepped back up onto his dais. "Take the fighters to the arena." He sat in his high-backed chair. "Let's calculate the odds and open up the betting!"

David shot Victor one last pleading look before he was escorted toward the penthouse elevators along with Pierce. Dawson trailed, likely so he could see the fight ringside. Victor ground his teeth. He wished Alexander had picked him to fight Pierce, to spare his friend the crisis of conscience he was facing.

Conscience.

Did Victor have one of those? He often wondered. He'd seen David kill, the man likely had killed nearly as much as Victor himself had, but it didn't bother Victor, not like it did David.

I suppose I have you to thank for that, Uncle Simon.

"Come here, Victor," Alexander called.

Victor stepped up the dais and stood by Alexander's chair.

"Tell me how the operation went."

It was fascinating to Victor how Alexander could shift his persona so easily. One minute he was the entertaining, crowd-pleasing, showman, and the next he was the shrewd businessman. He was two entirely different people somehow packaged in the same expensive suit.

Victor relayed the details of what happened and how Sandoval nearly botched the whole thing. He altered the details of what occurred with Agent Griffin to place the blame for Sandoval's death on him. "They had shot each other in the struggle." Victor also made no mention of how he'd called emergency services to Griffin's aid. Alexander didn't need to know that particular detail. Victor wasn't worried about witnesses; the only ones who'd been there were David and Dawson, and both were loyal to him. Well, Pierce had been there too, but he was about to die. And Victor knew Jordan's – he scoffed at the name – pride would limit who knew about what Victor did to save him.

Victor'd just finished his report when the announcer on the screen drew Alexander's attention.

"Ladies and gentlemen! Tonight, we have a special, unscheduled event!"

David appeared on-screen, shirtless and shouldering a champion's belt. He looked every bit the prize fighter, but with none of the swagger or braggadocio. His frown made it obvious he didn't want to be there.

"Give it up for the return of SPINE SPLITTER SADLER!"

The televised audience roared with delight.

"Facing him, for the prize of his own life, CPA, Casey Pierce."

Pierce's name was met with jeers and shouts of obscenities. The little man was likewise shirtless, exposing his scarecrow-like frame of skin and bone. He covered his head as paper cups and rolled up balls of greasy foil rained down on him.

Someone took David's champion belt from him and admitted him through a gate in the chain-link fence into the arena. Pierce had to be shoved into the octagon upon which he whirled and frantically tried to get back out, making it difficult for the staff to close and lock the gate.

The bell rang, and Pierce turned slowly to face David, who stood as still as a statue, staring at Pierce. The audience screamed and hollered, encouraging David to attack Pierce and dispatch him in a number of creative ways, but David merely stood, his expression doing nothing to hide the conflict raging within.

"Why isn't he doing anything?" Alexander asked.

"He doesn't think it's a fair fight," Victor answered.

Alexander scoffed. "Of course it isn't fair. It's not even a fight. It's an execution."

"He knows that."

Alexander shot a pointed look at Victor. "Does he need reminding that if he lets Pierce live, he forfeits his own life?"

And if you try to kill my friend, I'll gun you down on your throne in front of all your sycophantic leeches.

"I assure you. David will take care of Pierce."

As though David heard Victor's words, he strode over to Pierce, gripped his head with both hands, and sharply jerked it to the side, snapping his neck. Pierce crumpled into a heap, and the crowd exploded into raucous jeering. Apparently, they'd wanted David to prolong Pierce's suffering and were now angry their sadistic appetites had been denied.

"See?" Victor motioned to the screen.

Alexander frowned. "He couldn't have toyed with him a little first?"

Victor didn't answer.

Alexander waved him away. "Have the body disposed of."

"Any preference on where and how?"

Alexander hesitated and then said, "Send his head back to the FBI. I don't care what you do with the rest."

Victor nodded and stepped down from the dais. Dawson intercepted him, but before he could speak, Victor said, "The body's yours. I just need the head."

Dawson smiled and left. Victor turned back to face the wall of screens. David was climbing through the portal in the chain-link fence. He pushed away someone trying to drape the champion's belt on him and ignored the shouting of the crowd. Victor knew his friend wouldn't be sleeping this night.

He's weak, Uncle Simon whispered.

He's not a monster like you, Victor mentally answered.

You mean like us.

Is not justice a divine attribute of God? Is He not a God of vengeance? Then if we are to be as He is, should not that attribute be a part of His servants? Should we not seek justice?

JOURNAL OF FATHER KEVIN ALLEN DRAKES

CHAPTER
THREE

JORDAN WOKE when the EMTs arrived and was conscious for the ambulance ride and most of the hospital intake. He didn't really lose time until he was rushed into emergency surgery where they put him out so the doctors could operate. Miguel's gun had discharged point blank at his abdomen where his vest didn't cover. Miraculously, the round didn't pierce any vital organs, but it did nick his bowel, requiring surgery and a whole lot of antibiotics. Time to receiving medical attention had been a critical factor, the longer it took, the more toxic fluids would've leaked into Jordan's bloodstream, making Victor Reese's inexplicable call to 9-1-1 the defining act that would lead to the best possible recovery scenario. He had Reese to thank for helping him avoid sepsis, and possibly saving his life.

That infuriated Jordan.

He awoke from surgery to find his wife holding a foam cup filled with ice. She was rubbing a cube on his dry lips. "Jordan?"

"Kate," Jordan croaked, his throat sore from the intubation.

Tears poured down Kate's face as she planted a long kiss on his forehead. She spilled the ice, frozen cubes shattering and exploding all over the white tile floor.

Jordan forced a smile. "You dropped your ice."

Kate pulled away and glanced at the floor. She put the cup on a bedside tray and then sobbed, "I was on duty when they brought you in."

Jordan's smile faded as he took in her purple scrubs. "I'm sorry, sweetheart."

Kate wiped her eyes and nodded. "I'm just glad it wasn't more serious."

"Me too," Jordan agreed. Then it all came back to him. The motorcade, the explosions, Miguel's betrayal, Reese shooting his partner, and then… "Pierce!"

Jordan tried to sit up, but pressure in his right side alerted him to his condition and he froze. There wasn't pain yet, the morphine drip saw to that, though Jordan knew there would be in the days to come–pain of all kinds. And he knew, even before having a chance to fight the urge, what he would do to dull that pain. He was going to relapse. It wasn't a fear, or even a temptation, just a fact as evident as the morning sun shining through the windows.

"None of that." Kate pressed a hand to the top of his chest and forced him to lie back. "Who's Pierce?"

"An asset we were taking to the airport."

"Can you tell me what happened?" Kate asked.

"Probably not."

She nodded. She was wonderful that way. She knew and accepted that there were things Jordan wasn't allowed to talk about, and she respected that. But this time was different. This time his work had come crashing into her world. He could only imagine the shock of being on duty when the ambulance rushed him into *her* hospital's emergency room. She deserved to know more.

"Our motorcade was attacked on the interstate. We lost some agents and the asset we were protecting. Miguel..." Jordan's voice faltered. "He's dead," was all he could manage.

"Oh no." Kate's tears intensified. "What are Marta and the kids gonna do?"

Jordan ground his teeth. Miguel's crime would cost him his benefits. His wife and children would get nothing.

A knock at the door stopped Kate from asking more questions. A moment later Jordan's superior, Special Agent in Charge Thomas Morrison, entered.

Jordan tried to sit up, but Kate stopped him again.

Morrison waved a hand. "It's okay, Jordan."

He relaxed. "Sir."

Morrison slid his rectangular glasses back up his nose with his index finger. He smiled at Kate. "How you holding up, Kate?"

Kate rose and gave Morrison a quick hug. "I'm okay."

"Good." Morrison motioned at Jordan. "You mind if I have a minute with your husband?"

Kate met Jordan's eyes and flashed a smile. "Sure."

"Thank you," Morrison said as Kate left the room. He waited for the door to shut and then took a seat next to Jordan's bed.

"Alexander has Pierce," Jordan growled. "He's probably dead already."

Morrison removed his glasses, folded them, and put them in his suitcoat pocket. "The field office reported receiving a box with Pierce's head in it early this morning. They left it at our front door."

Jordan clenched his fists. Pierce had been the key to taking down Alexander's syndicate. As his personal accountant, Pierce had been privy to all the man's financial dealings, both legal and extra-legal. If money was involved, so was Pierce. Consequently, the man knew everything about Alexander's operation. Well, not everything; Pierce hadn't known Miguel was on the take.

"My partner tried to kill me," Jordan blurted out.

"I've been briefed on what you told the agents that found you. You didn't tell them who shot Sandoval, though."

"Victor Reese," Jordan said, and it came out sounding like a growl. "Apparently my insistence that I ride with Pierce fouled up their plan. Reese executed Miguel for complicating things."

Jordan was surprised at the guilt that boiled up in him for that. He'd insisted on riding with Pierce. And even though his partner had tried to kill him, he couldn't help but feel his actions caused Miguel's death. It was insane. Love, hate, and grief all tangled inside him in a maddening knot. He bit down on his jaw to prevent a sob.

Morrison sighed. "OPR is going to want to talk to you. They're going to be asking you some tough questions and digging into your life."

"They think *I* was in on it?" Jordan barked out a disbelieving laugh.

Morrison hesitated. "People are already talking. You were Miguel's partner and his friend, after all."

"And he shot me!"

"I know."

A spear of anxiety stabbed Jordan's chest. "Tom, *you* don't think I had a part in this?"

"Of course not, but I wanted you to hear it from me in person. You are as of this moment on investigative leave." Morrison stood and gently put a hand on Jordan's shoulder. "But I've got your back, Jordan. I know the kind of agent you are. I know you'd sooner die than take a bribe or put your fellow agents in danger. I'm ready to fight by your side the whole way, and I promise we'll get this all sorted out."

Jordan nodded, not daring to look at Morrison for fear he would see his tears.

"I'll let you get some rest," Morrison said, and then left the room.

Jordan waited for the sound of the door latching and then he hit the siderail of his hospital bed. And then he hit it again. And then again and continued hitting it until it broke free and hung off the bed's frame at an odd angle. The destruction triggered alarms, and a beat later Kate rushed in, followed by another nurse.

"Jordan?!" Kate called, a note of panic in her voice.

He didn't answer. He needed a drink. He needed one bad.

I didn't come to this in a moment. These questions, these doubts had been simmering for a long time. But there was one case that put me over the edge. A young man who'd been raping his neighbor's seven-year-old son confessed everything to me in horrific detail. I pled with him to turn himself in, to get help, but was not legally able to do much more. But that wasn't the worst thing he was guilty of...

JOURNAL OF FATHER KEVIN ALLEN DRAKES

CHAPTER
FOUR

VICTOR MOTIONED for David to pull the car over and park it on a dimly lit street. David veered right, lined the car up against the curb, and cut the lights. Directly across the street from where they parked was a large, Victorian-style mansion. Its iron gates were no longer black, time and weather having eroded the metal and encrusted a good portion of the fence in rust. A "No Trespassing" sign hung askew over a chained and pad-locked front gate. The doors and windows of the mansion were boarded up, and the grounds were overgrown with unkempt grass and weeds.

"Why are we here?" David shifted the car into park. "I hate this place."

"We're here to remember."

David rubbed his eyes. "Remember what? The beatings? The hunger? The abuse?"

"No." Victor scrutinized the front courtyard, trying to see the ghosts of children at play. "To remember where we came from."

"My best memory of this hell hole was when we took Anne and ran away."

Anne, scoffed Uncle Simon.

"It *was* bad, David, but also momentous."

David shook his head. "What's this about, Victor?"

Victor looked away from the crumbling mansion. "I know you find much of what we do distasteful."

"You mean like snapping the neck of a defenseless, skinny-ass accountant?"

"I didn't know Edward was planning that, I swear it."

David gripped the steering wheel tightly. "You aren't the one who has to carry that on his conscience."

"David, I'm sorry. I really am."

David shut off the car. "You say we've come a long way from this place, Victor, but have we? We ran away to escape the violence and to be free. The violence followed us, and I don't feel very free."

"No." Victor looked back at the mansion–their former home. "We aren't free. Not yet."

"Yet?"

Great setup. Now reel him in, Uncle Simon whispered.

Victor turned back and met David's eyes. "Edward Alexander's been in power so long that he's lost something very important."

"What's that?"

"Fear. He's not afraid anymore."

David leaned back in his seat. "Why should he be afraid? He's the most powerful man in Lake Side."

"And what gives him that power in which he is so secure?"

David shrugged. "His enforcers. We make sure what he wants done gets done, and we punish those who cross him."

"So, who has the *real* power?" Victor let that hang.

David's jaw tightened. "You want to depose him."

"Not me." Victor put a hand on David's shoulder. "Us! You and I can take Edward down and then run things how we want to." He motioned excitedly. "Think about it! We could end blood sports and child trafficking, or anything else we find distasteful! We would control everything!"

David slowly nodded. "We could kill him at any time, but you know it's more complicated than just putting a bullet in his head. The underbosses would tear the syndicate apart trying to fill the power vacuum. Most have their own cadre of enforcers. How do you do this without starting a city-wide gang war?"

"We convince Edward the underbosses are plotting against him, give him back his fear but poison it so it becomes paranoia. Then we encourage him to consolidate all of the syndicate's enforcers under his direct rule with me as his lieutenant. After that we simply wait for the right opportunity."

David frowned. "It could work. But how do we make him think his underbosses are plotting against him?"

Victor sighed. "I'm working that out. I just need to know that when the time comes, you'll support me."

"Of course I will. Victor, you and Anne are the only people in the world I care about. I will always have your back."

Victor smiled. He knew David would support him. He always had. But instead of looking relieved, David looked troubled.

"What is it?" Victor asked.

"Is this all there is?"

"What do you mean?" Victor furrowed his brow.

David stared at the condemned mansion. "Violence and pain. Are we meant to forever be men of blood?"

Victor rolled his eyes. "Have you been reading Nietzsche again?"

David smiled. "A little."

"Look, David." Victor gripped his friend's shoulder. "I don't know if this is all there is or if there's more. What I do know is that we've suffered a lot, and we've had to fight for every scrap of freedom we have. Life hasn't been kind to us, and we've had to fight and, yes, kill, just to survive, and we're going to have to spill more blood if we want to thrive. It's ugly, but it's the truth."

"I know, I'm just tired of it." David patted Victor's hand, and he removed it.

"I understand. Just hang in there a little longer until we take what's rightfully ours, and then you can rest."

David sighed. "Can we just get out of here?"

Victor nodded, confused that David hadn't snapped out of his melancholy, but he didn't want to press the issue. They rode in silence back to Victor's apartment where David dropped him off. Victor entered the swanky high rise and wove through the crowd milling about the lobby until he reached the elevators. He pressed the call button and waited with head down until the car arrived.

Although the elevator was empty, the mirrored interior created a disorienting replicating effect that made Victor feel as though he wasn't alone. He swiped his keycard and pressed the button that would take him to the penthouse, then leaned against the corner.

Something about David's reaction, or non-reaction, to his plot to overthrow Alexander bothered him. David said he was with him, but Victor didn't feel it. And what was David holding back? What was he hiding?

"David is weak." A tall, pale-faced man dressed all in black appeared in the reflection next to him.

Victor fell backward, drawing a handgun from inside his jacket in pure reflex. He aimed it at the mirrored wall, but the tall, pale man was gone.

The elevator chimed and the doors opened. Victor lowered his weapon and ran a hand through his wavy hair. He backed out of the elevator, unwilling to turn his back on the mirrored wall where a moment earlier he had seen, *actually seen*, his Uncle Simon.

Lights automatically woke as Victor entered his penthouse. He holstered his gun and removed his suitcoat. He tossed the black jacket on the back of a white chair and made for the kitchen. There he threw open a cupboard and grabbed a tall glass. A different cupboard contained a cask of amber liquid. Victor filled his glass and drank the whiskey down as quick as he could, grimacing as it burned his throat but refusing to pause. He slammed the glass down on the marble counter so hard that it cracked.

Had he really just *seen* Uncle Simon? Sure, he mentally heard his uncle's commentary sometimes, but Victor thought that was a trauma response–an echo constructed by his own damaged psyche.

Victor stripped off his shirt as he made his way to his bedroom where he slammed the door and approached a tall, narrow window. He stared out at the city. The cityscape at night always calmed his nerves, and after a minute the soothing effect of the night-time view blanketed him. He rested his head against the glass and took deep, deliberate breaths.

"You can't run from me, Jonny." Uncle Simon appeared behind Victor in the window's reflection.

Victor launched himself back, grabbed the lamp from the nightstand next to his bed, and hurled it at the specter. The lamp exploded into a dozen pieces, leaving a stark crack in the window, but Uncle Simon merely smiled. Victor's bed stopped his retreat, and he fell backwards onto the mattress. He rolled off, trying to stand back up, but fell to the floor. "Just leave me alone!"

But the tall, pale man was gone.

Victor slumped. Was he going crazy? There was no way he was really seeing his uncle.

"Why won't you just leave me alone?"

Victor trembled as someone knelt next to him on the floor. He didn't dare look up for fear of seeing that wicked smile.

"Because," Uncle Simon whispered, "I chose you to continue my work."

Victor shook his head, slapping his temple once, twice, and continuing until he saw stars and the pain forced him to stop. "I'm not like you..."

Uncle Simon embraced him, his hot breath whispering in Victor's ear, "Not yet."

It was in this moment of despair that God sent me someone who could do what I could not—a knight to battle the dragon. A hero with a sense of justice like my own. Someone who would do what was needed to stop the evil. An avenging angel in the form of Agent Jordan Griffin.

JOURNAL OF FATHER KEVIN ALLEN DRAKES

CHAPTER
FIVE

EIGHT WEEKS LATER...

JORDAN'S GUNSHOT had healed quickly, so quickly in fact that he'd only spent a couple weeks in the hospital. Unfortunately, he'd only made it one day at home before getting blackout drunk. Kate found him passed out upon returning from her late shift. To Jordan's surprise, she'd gone easy on him. That was almost worse than her crying and yelling.

And then there was Marta, Miguel's widow. She blamed Jordan for her husband's death. It was easier for her to believe the persistent rumors that Jordan had conspired to kill Miguel instead of the truth. Jordan was dead to Marta, his status of godfather to their children unceremoniously revoked. That, of course, led to more drinking, which led to more disappointment in his wife's eyes, and Jordan was again attending Alcoholics Anonymous meetings.

The only bright spot was that the day had finally come for Jordan to return to work. He pushed open the glass door and entered an open floor filled with cubicles. He was met with a shout, and then applause. Agents stood and clapped as he made his way toward SAC Morrison's office. Jordan forced a smile and waved.

It was a nice gesture of support on his first day back in the office, but how many of these people really believed he wasn't on the take? How many were just pretending? Did anyone believe he hadn't killed Miguel and turned over Pierce?

He made it to Morrison's office door and gave one more wave to the room as the applause tapered off. He knocked, but Morrison had already seen him through the window and was motioning him into the office. Jordan opened the door and stepped in.

"Sir, did you put them up to..." Jordan trailed off.

He hadn't noticed the two other people sitting in Morrison's office. The first was his favorite authoritarian asshole, Assistant Special Agent in Charge Adam Seigers. The balding, overweight bureaucrat was surreptitiously ogling the other guest in Morrison's office: a young, raven-haired woman dressed in a smart charcoal pant suit. She'd been hidden from Jordan's view by the positioning of her chair–whether deliberate or not, Jordan couldn't guess.

Morrison motioned to the woman. "This is Agent Danielle Kelly. She's a profiler working homicide."

Agent Kelly stood. "Good to meet you, Agent Griffin." She extended her hand.

Jordan gave her a perfunctory handshake and then said to Morrison, "I can come back later."

"No." Morrison shook his head. "Please, take a seat."

Jordan forced another smile, walked to the remaining empty seat set opposite Morrison's desk—in between Seigers and Kelly–and sat in time with Agent Kelly.

Jordan nodded at Seigers who replied unenthusiastically, "Griffin."

"Agent Kelly just transferred from Chicago." Morrison smiled at the woman who couldn't have been older than thirty. "She's something of a rising star in the bureau. Made her name solving cold cases."

Agent Kelly laughed. "I'm just a true crime buff with a badge. Honestly, I'm thrilled to be here because I'm absolutely *obsessed* with Lake Side's own premiere serial killer, the Mad Reaper."

Jordan stiffened as a parade of images came to him unbidden: *the man with the scythe and the skull mask, a naked Barbie with tangled hair, an old travel trunk and a well, and a butcher knife covered in blood.*

"Thanatos," Jordan mumbled.

Agent Kelly cocked a manicured eyebrow. "What was that?"

Jordan shifted in his chair. "He called himself Thanatos."

Agent Kelly leaned toward Jordan. "That name came from his only surviving victim. It wasn't ever made public. How'd you know that?"

Jordan's jaw tightened. "I looked into the case once, unofficially."

Before Agent Kelly could ask any more questions, Jordan shifted his focus to Morrison. "Sir? What's going on here?"

"Agent Kelly is your new partner, Griffin," Seigers said with a cruel grin.

Jordan glanced at Seigers, then the woman, and finally at Morrison. "The task force needs a profiler?"

Morrison frowned. "You're being reassigned, Jordan. We're moving you off organized crime to homicide."

"What?" Jordan stood so fast he knocked over his chair. He slammed his palms down on Morrison's desk. "Tom, you can't do this to me!"

Seigers stood and put a hand on Jordan's shoulder. "Watch it, Griffin."

"Get your hand off me, Seigers," Jordan growled.

Agent Kelly stared at them, eyes wide and mouth agape.

"Or what?" Seigers sneered.

Jordan threw off Seigers' hand, spun around, and glared at him.

"You're going to show your SAC some respect, Agent Griffin!" Seigers shouted, but it carried a note of uncertainty. Jordan had shaken him.

Morrison glanced at the stunned woman. "Agent Kelly, would you mind giving us a minute?"

The young woman nodded, gathered up her bag, and hurried from the room.

"Sit down, Jordan," Morrison ordered.

Morrison glanced at his ASAC and said, "Adam, can you go check on Agent Kelly for me? Make sure she's all right?"

"Sure." Seigers stared Jordan down as he left the room.

Jordan retrieved his chair and sat. "Why, Tom?"

Morrison massaged his forehead. "It's complicated."

"Someone up the chain thinks I'm dirty? Thinks I can't be trusted?"

Morrison sighed. "Maybe. But that's not what this is about."

"Then why sideline me?" Again, Jordan came up out of his chair.

"It's not just *you*. The task force is being disbanded. We took our shot with Pierce and missed. That operation wasn't cheap. It cost us money and political capital, and now the deputy director wants us to shift our focus."

Jordan balled his fists. "Away from dismantling the biggest criminal syndicate in American history?"

"No," Morrison said with obvious forced patience, "away from investigating a *legitimate businessman*."

"That's bullshit and you know it!"

"Agent Griffin!" Morrison snapped.

Jordan met his eyes and sat back in his chair.

Morrison drew in a calming breath. "Since the Pierce debacle, Edward Alexander has made some new friends—wealthy, influential people who run in the same circles as the deputy director. People like Senator Garcia and Senator Chandry, and let's not leave out Congressman Jennings. Those three have persuaded the deputy director to make this decision."

Jordan shook his head. "They're wrong. Can't we go to the director, or petition the AG to—"

"Read between the lines, Jordan!" Morrison shouted, real anger in his voice.

The verbal slap shook Jordan, and it took a beat for him to recover before realization dawned on him. "Alexander's gotten to the deputy director."

Morrison slumped forward, eyes downcast, elbows leaning on his desk as he held the sides of his head. He looked utterly defeated. "We scared him. Despite all his precautions, conspiracies, and power, we came too close. As a result, he had to up his game to protect his empire." Morrison looked up into Jordan's eyes. "He beat us, Jordan. Alexander beat us. It's over."

JORDAN STARED up at the skyscrapers looming over the center of Lakeside. One of those stood out among the others, Axum Tower, Edward Alexander's glass monolith. It was the office building from which he ran his operation as well as a multimillion-dollar prop he used to masquerade as a *legitimate businessman.*

Jordan ground his teeth, something he did more and more often lately. His smartwatch chimed, and he glanced at it. The notification was a message from Kate asking if he was okay.

He ignored it.

They'd started arguing again, or rather, he was being an asshole and she was losing patience with him. She'd gotten upset with him before she'd left earlier that evening.

"I could drive you to your meeting," Kate offered.

Jordan sat at the kitchen table with his arms folded. He shook his head.

"Listen, I'm sorry I have to work late again. We're short-staffed, especially with Trish leaving, but I put in for a shift change and Laney promised I was on the short list."

Jordan shrugged.

"Say something!" Kate shouted.

Jordan looked at her. "Like what?"

"Anything!" Kate stood from the table and grabbed her keys and purse. "I just want you to talk to me!"

"I've got nothing to say."

Kate stared at him, tears spilling out of her brown eyes. "Why do I even try?" She left the kitchen, slamming the door on her way out.

Jordan knew what he was doing. He was drowning in liquor and despair and was dragging Kate down with him. He knew what he was doing, and he couldn't stop himself.

He stopped in front of a towering cathedral. It was a beautiful building, easily a hundred years old, built in the gothic architecture style popular more than a century earlier, complete with spires and large stained-glass windows.

Tonight he'd elected to walk to his AA meeting instead of driving, ostensibly because the summer night air helped him cope, when in fact he just didn't want the burden of his Jeep should he decide to stop at a bar on the way home. With Kate working the night shift, relapse was all but certain.

Jordan climbed the stone steps and opened one of the two large, ornate doors. He slipped into the chapel annex, glancing into the vast sanctuary as he made to take a right into the stairwell that descended to the basement where his meeting would be held. Jordan hesitated as he watched a priest sitting in the pew next to a man in an oversized camouflaged coat. They were talking, and the man kept his head bowed. The priest placed an arm around him and patted him on the back before standing and walking away.

Before Jordan knew it, he had stepped into the sanctuary and was walking down the aisle in between pews. He stopped at the altar and looked up at a large crucifix with a likeness of Jesus of Nazareth hanging from the cross, complete with crown of thorns.

"Can I help you?"

Jordan turned to find the priest approaching him. He was younger than most but older than Jordan by ten years at least.

"I don't think anyone can," Jordan said. "Not even The Lord."

"The Lord isn't just *anyone*." The priest flashed a good-natured smirk. "He's God. He's kind of good at everything."

The man in the camouflaged coat rose. Behind the long hair and unkempt beard was a face much younger than Jordan had assumed–the face of a man in his late twenties. Their eyes met for a moment, and Jordan recognized that haunted look. It was the look of someone who'd truly tasted hell. Jordan knew that look. He'd seen it in the mirror.

The priest nodded at the homeless man. "God be with you, Kyle."

The man, Kyle, glanced at the priest, nodded, then quickly left.

The priest turned back to Jordan. "Now, you were about to tell me how you are a lost cause?"

Jordan looked at the priest. "I'm sorry, Father..."

"Drakes." Father Drakes extended his hand. "Kevin Drakes."

Jordan shook Father Drakes' hand. "I should let you get back to your business." Jordan made to leave, embarrassed that he'd even come into the sanctuary and bothered the priest.

"I've seen you here before."

Jordan halted his retreat.

"You're part of the AA group that meets downstairs."

Jordan tightened his jaw. "I'm Jordan."

Father Drakes inclined his head. "Well, Jordan, why don't you unburden yourself?" He motioned to a nearby confessional.

Jordan shook his head. "I'm afraid I'm not Catholic."

Father Drakes chuckled. "Catholics aren't the only sinners in the world, though we're quite good at it."

Jordan smiled. He was starting to like Father Drakes. The man's self-deprecating humor was charming, and he had a trustworthy face.

"Come. Confession is good for the soul." Before Jordan could protest further, Father Drakes walked to the confessional and opened the closet-like door.

Jordan drew in a deep breath. "Okay."

He entered the parishioner's side of the confessional as Father Drakes entered the priest's side. Jordan sat on a bench and glanced at the wood lattice screen where he could see Father Drakes' profile. "So how does this work?"

"Well, the ritual starts with—"

"Forgive me Father for I have sinned?" Jordan finished.

Father Drakes chuckled. "Yes. And then just tell me it's your first confession and talk about what's bothering you."

Jordan cleared his throat. "Forgive me Father, for I have sinned. This is my first confession, and I have..." Jordan shifted uncomfortably on the wooden bench. "I'm a drunk—an alcoholic."

"So, I guessed." Father Drakes chuckled, but it wasn't unkind.

Jordan responded with a nervous laugh of his own. "Yeah, I suppose that one's obvious."

"What else burdens your soul?"

Jordan was about to confess his lack of motivation to stop drinking and all the lying to Kate that went with it, but it felt wrong. Oh, it was true. He didn't have all that much in the way of motivation right now, and he *was* lying to Kate, others, and himself. But that wasn't what this was about. Those were symptoms. Manifestations of something deeper, something darker.

Thanatos.

He'd never told anyone about *that*. He opened his mouth to speak, but nothing came out. It was almost as if Thanatos were still with him, watching him, threatening him, and Jordan couldn't reveal that monster's atrocities without confessing his own.

An old travel trunk. A crumbling stone well.

Father Drakes hadn't nudged him, and Jordan appreciated the priest's deft insight, but Jordan decided to change tack. He couldn't talk about The Mad Reaper. Not today.

"I'm a federal agent, Father, and I've also been a soldier. I've seen evil, real evil. I've dedicated my life to fighting it. But…" Hot tears stung the corners of Jordan's eyes. "It's all pointless. None of it makes any difference."

"I'm sure that's not true, Jordan," Father Drakes soothed.

"Don't patronize me!" Jordan shouted, then he froze. Where had that come from? "I'm sorry, Father. I don't know why I said that."

"It's okay, Jordan. Your anger tells me you're being truthful. Please continue."

Jordan sucked in a breath. "A crime lord rules this city, Father. His name is Edward Alexander. All of Lake Side's organized crime is under his purview: drugs, prostitution, gambling, counterfeiting, murder. You name it. He rose to power years ago when he united all of Lake Side's crime families into a single organization that we dubbed 'The Underground Empire.' He has an endless fortune and powerful friends at every level of government. I've been trying to bring him down for years, and I almost did it. We arrested his accountant—a scrawny, pathetic man named Casey Pierce. Though that coward of a man turned out to be incredibly brave, albeit his motives were mostly self-preservation. He agreed to testify against Alexander, and he could've brought the whole thing down. He had names and records. He knew everything."

"What happened?" Father Drakes asked.

Jordan ground his teeth. "My partner was dirty. He shot me and gave Pierce to Alexander's enforcers. Then they killed my partner and sent us Pierce's head."

"Good heavens."

Jordan choked out a bitter laugh. "And today, I found out that Alexander has corrupted our deputy director, the man who calls the shots for our investigation. Suffice it to say, there is no more investigation. Alexander won."

"Ye have said, It is vain to serve God: and what profit is it that we have kept his ordinance, and that we have walked mournfully before the Lord of hosts? And now we call the proud happy; yea, they that work wickedness are set up; yea, they that tempt God are even delivered," Father Drakes recited. "Malachi, chapter three."

"What does that mean?" Jordan asked.

"It means injustice is part of this life, but the rest of the passage goes on to explain that ultimately, God will set things right."

Tears spilled down Jordan's cheeks. "I can't wait for God to do it."

Silence.

Had he offended the priest? Jordan looked through the screen. "Father?"

Father Drakes sighed. "Can I make a confession of my own, Jordan?"

Not being Catholic, Jordan had no idea if this was normal, though his instincts told him it wasn't. "Of course, Father."

"Please, just call me Kevin. Catholic though I am, I'm not much for standing on ceremony."

"Okay, Kevin."

Father Drakes—Kevin—briefly smiled. "I'm having a crisis of faith of my own right now. I am supposed to aid the almighty in comforting his children and absolving them of their sins. I take confession, but what people sometimes misunderstand is that repentance isn't just confessing. That's just the beginning. They must strive to change. And I understand that change can take time, especially with addictive behaviors, but..."

"But what?" Jordan prompted.

"Some sins are so grievous, so ugly, and some sinners so immersed in evil..." Kevin faltered. "I believe in God's mercy, Jordan, I really do, but the same God who was the gentle man from Galilee, isn't he also the same God who destroyed Sodom and Gomorrah?"

Jordan didn't know how to answer that. He wasn't a theologian. He hadn't even read the Old Testament. But then again, he didn't think Kevin was really asking him, so he stayed quiet and let the priest continue.

"Justice is the other side of that divine coin. I'm supposed to love people even when they are demons wearing men's faces, even when they tell me they've done horrific things. Even when I know they're going to *do* horrific things."

"You know I'm a federal agent, Kevin," Jordan said. "Are you trying to report a crime?"

"The Sacred Seal of Confession, and the law, says I can't."

"I understand." Jordan ran a hand through his hair. He really needed a drink.

"That being said," Kevin continued, "I can't continue with this on my conscience." He sighed. "There is a young man whose father is a powerful politician. He came to me months ago, confessing to being a child predator. I advised him to turn himself in, and he did. Charges were brought, but the prosecutor suddenly dropped the charges, and the young man went free."

"The same kind of corruption I've seen, to be sure," Jordan said. "But it sounds like you did what you could."

"No," Kevin said. "I advised him to tell the police everything he'd done. He only told them about molesting a few neighborhood boys."

Jordan frowned. "I don't understand."

"He told me," Kevin's voice cracked, "that he'd strangled a five-year-old to death and buried him in Turner Grove on the southside of the lake. He came to me because he was tempted to do it again."

"You're sure it's not a false confession?"

"I found a news story about a missing undocumented boy named Jorge Torres," Kevin's voice faltered again. "The dates and details lined up with what this man told me."

Ice formed in Jordan's stomach and quickly washed through his extremities. He clenched his jaw, and the chill was quickly replaced by burning anger. *Jorge.* An illegal immigrant. That hit a little too close to home.

"He *will* kill again, Jordan. And knowing this, I am expected to do nothing? God expects me to love this monster and not prevent him from killing another child?"

"Give me a name," Jordan growled.

Kevin snapped his head up and looked at Jordan through the confessional screen. "It's against the law for me—"

"I'm not talking about taking it to the law, the law failed!" Jordan snapped. "And I won't stand by and let any more innocent people get hurt because we adhere to *law* while others ignore it. They aren't playing by the rules, Kevin. And if we're to have any chance of beating them, we can't be bound by those rules either."

The priest stared at Jordan through the screen. His mouth hung open in shock. Truth be told, Jordan was just as shocked at what he'd said, but the words felt good, they felt *right.*

"Jordan, I can't…"

"He's going to kill another child!" Jordan slid closer to the screen. "He told you that himself. Do you think God just wants us to let that happen?"

The priest was silent for a long time, and when he opened his mouth to speak, Jordan was expecting him to tell him to leave, but instead he asked, "You'll remedy this yourself? Secretly and outside the law?"

"Yes," Jordan answered, and something inside him slid into place, as though he'd just found the missing piece of a puzzle. It numbed his pain with a potency stronger than any liquor.

"Then I will give you the name on two conditions."

"And those are?"

Kevin looked away from the screen. "First, you are to return to me and 'confess' what you've done. I will absolve you of your sin, and I must know what happens."

"Okay."

Kevin looked back at Jordan through the screen. "And second, you must not kill this man. As much for your own sake as his. Whatever else you do to stop him, you cannot cross that line."

But I've already crossed it. An image of him holding a bloody knife flashed across his mind.

Jordan clenched his fists. "How else am I supposed to stop him?"

"You'll think of something. Now, promise me, or you don't get the name." The genial priest sounded surprisingly tough. "Vengeance is mine saith The Lord. We can't do this for revenge, we have to do this only to protect others."

A disappointment settled on Jordan, and that disturbed him. Why was he so eager to kill? He checked his bloodlust by embracing Kevin's non-lethal condition with a desperately sincere, "I promise."

A hesitation in the priest told Jordan that Kevin had picked up on his inner turmoil. Nevertheless, he spoke the name, "Evan Chandry."

"As in Senator Chandry? Evan is his son?"

"I told you his father was a powerful politician."

"Senator Chandry is one of the politicians in Alexander's pocket–one of the senators leaning on the deputy director to shutter my task force."

Kevin crossed himself and muttered something Jordan couldn't quite hear, but apparently the priest was thinking the same thing as Jordan. This couldn't be a coincidence. This was a sign from God. This was how he was supposed to fight the plague of corruption infecting the city. And as icing on the cake, Jordan would get to strike back at the dirty senator who'd taken away his power to fight the Underground Empire by hurting his son.

Jordan jumped to his feet and threw open the confessional door.

Kevin followed him out. "Wait!"

Jordan paused and turned back.

"What are you going to do?" Kevin asked, his face pale, drained of blood.

"I'm going to stop him." With that, Jordan turned and strode up the carpeted incline between the pews. He left the cathedral, a sense of serene focus cooling his burning desire to drink. He didn't need alcohol. He'd found something much, much more satisfying.

By the laws of man and the church what we were doing was wrong. But in my heart it felt right. It felt like God's will. Though frightened that'd we'd be found out and lose everything, I had a relief of conscience and peace that I hadn't known for weeks.

JOURNAL OF FATHER KEVIN ALLEN DRAKES

CHAPTER
SIX

VICTOR STOOD BEHIND and to the right of Edward Alexander's highbacked wicker chair. It was a sunny morning, one perfect for taking brunch on the lavishly furnished porch of Alexander's country club. Victor didn't usually play the role of stoic, menacing bodyguard, but this was a special occasion—a first in-person meet between Alexander and the head of the La Sangre Cartel, a grizzled, chewed-up looking veteran guerilla named Naolin Escarra.

La Sangre was Juarez's counterpart to Lake Side's "Underground Empire," and this partnership had been in the works for over two years. Victor knew his assignment of standing behind his boss and looking dangerous was just the dick-measuring contest mob bosses liked to engage in when they met with potential partners, but the practice was rooted in underworld savvy. You wanted to send a message to the man sitting opposite you that if the negotiations went poorly, you were ready to bring your most effective force to bear. Paranoid though it might seem, violence was always a possibility when meeting with men like Escarra, and Victor was Alexander's most dangerous soldier.

If only he knew what you were really capable of, Uncle Simon said.

Victor squeezed his eyes shut, his mirrored sunglasses hiding his pained look. *Jenny says I don't have to be like you, that it's my choice.*

Uncle Simon just laughed.

He hadn't *seen* Uncle Simon since that night in his penthouse two months ago, but the dead man's voice was getting louder, to the point of becoming more than just an internal thing. Victor was actually hearing it, and that frightened him.

Victor gritted his teeth and glanced at Escarra's bodyguard—also standing behind her boss's chair. It was a woman, which was strange in Victor's experience dealing with Latin culture; they tended to hold to more traditional gender roles.

The woman had chin-length hair, wore no sunglasses, and was dressed in a light-colored pant suit that well complimented her olive complexion. She wore no tie, and her blouse was unbuttoned just enough to show off a tasteful amount of cleavage. Victor marked that as a decision that was more tactical than fashionable. Although popular culture liked to depict women as the physical equal of men in battle, the truth was nature manufactured them smaller and weaker than males. In a fight, women had to rely on speed and strategy much more than men did. Distraction was an age-old tactic, one which women had long taken advantage of by leveraging their sex appeal.

The woman caught Victor staring at her.

He quickly looked away, not sure how she'd known it as he was hiding behind his sunglasses, but a slight smirk on her face confirmed to him that she *had* noticed.

Victor waited for the inevitable criticism to come from Uncle Simon, but there was no mocking laughter or jibe about his weakness. For the first time in weeks, Victor's mind was quiet. He risked another glance and found her staring back at him, a smile on her face.

Victor re-focused on Alexander and Escarra. They were both

speaking in the frantic cadence of fluent Spanish, and Victor had a bit of difficulty keeping up with the conversation. From what he could glean, the topic was shipment schedules and warehousing product in Lake Side.

Escarra brought up the sex trade and asked about secure housing for his girls, to which Alexander responded with a bawdy joke. Victor chuckled and then caught himself and covered it with a cough. Fortunately, neither Escarra nor Alexander had noticed the break from decorum. Escarra's bodyguard had, however. She narrowed her eyes at him, the smile disappearing from her face.

That stung for some reason, which thoroughly confused Victor. The joke had been distasteful and was made at the expense of the women being discussed who were, for all intents and purposes, sex-slaves, but why would the disapproval of Escarra's bodyguard matter one whit to Victor? Since when did he care what others thought of him?

For the rest of the meeting Victor didn't dare look at his counterpart. He kept his focus on Alexander and translating the conversation. He was relieved when the two men stood and shook hands.

"My associate, Victor Reese, will escort you to your car," Alexander said in English.

Victor took the cue and stepped forward. Escarra nodded at him, turned, and walked away, his enigmatic bodyguard staying a step behind him.

As they made their way down the causeway toward a waiting Rolls-Royce, the woman slowed so as to fall in step next to Victor. He tensed, and he had to fight the urge to reach for his weapon.

"¿Asi que hablas espanol?" She asked.

"A little," Victor replied in English.

"It would seem more than a little." The woman cast him a sidelong glance. "I'm Camilla."

Victor chuckled. "Clever. But, not your real name I take it?"

Camilla smiled. "Nothing gets past you, does it, *Victor*?"

The way she emphasized his name told him she'd guessed *Victor* wasn't his real name either.

This woman is dangerous. That thought sent a thrill through his chest.

"It is who I am now," he tersely replied.

"Fair enough."

They walked in silence for a beat before Victor felt compelled to ask, "Are you headed back to Juarez then?"

Camilla chuckled.

She knows you know their plans. You're terrible at idle chit-chat. The voice of reprimand wasn't Uncle Simon's, but his own. Awkward though Victor felt, that at least was comforting.

"We're staying in Lake Side while Papi works out the details of his agreement with your boss."

"Papi?" Victor laughed at that. "You call one of the most dangerous men in Mexico, 'Papi'?"

Camilla smiled. "He has all of his women attendants call him that, and he calls us his daughters."

"I'm sorry. I didn't mean to laugh. It just made me think of what Mr. Alexander would do if I called him *daddy*."

Camilla's controlled expression faltered, and she erupted into genuine laughter. She caught herself and coughed after Escarra cast a quizzical glance over his shoulder.

"You're a bad influence on me, Victor Reese."

Victor smiled at her use of his full name. For reasons he couldn't completely understand, it made him feel special.

They continued in friendly conversation until arriving at the curb and the waiting Rolls-Royce. The driver stood by the rear door and opened it for Escarra when the man drew close.

Panic brought Victor back to the moment. He'd been so wrapped up flirting with Camilla he'd actually forgotten the plan. He cast a wild glance at the tree line beyond the parking lot. He couldn't see him, but he knew Dawson was hiding there.

Escarra climbed into the backseat of the luxury car, and the driver glanced expectantly at Camilla.

Camilla stopped walking and turned to face him. "Well, Victor, it was a pleasure to—"

Victor grabbed her arm, pulled her toward him, pivoted, and launched both of them away from the Rolls-Royce to the side of the causeway where the manicured lawn would cushion their landing.

Heat, light, and deafening sound erupted behind them as the car exploded. A flaming tire landed a foot from Victor's head, and pieces of shrapnel *clanged* as they rained down all around them.

When it was over, Victor found himself lying on top of Camilla, her brown eyes wide. She looked from the flaming wreckage that was the Rolls-Royce, to him. Their eyes met, and something passed between them, a primal electricity, and though they were surrounded by debris, flames, and panicked shouts, Victor wanted to kiss her. He looked away, stood, and reached down to help her up. Camilla took his hand and he lifted her to her feet.

"Papi!" Camilla shouted and ran toward the wreckage.

Victor dusted himself off and cast a glance at the tree line. A bullet bike sped away in the distance, the whine of its engine soon drowned out by the sound of sirens.

Uncle Simon's voice finally returned, though it was quieter than normal, and wholly internal. *You should've let her die.*

Yes, Victor agreed. *But I didn't.*

I was worried he'd lose control and kill Evan, but I'd seen something in Jordan — honor. Yes, he was angry. Yes, he was haunted. But deep down I knew he was a good man and not a murderer.

JOURNAL OF FATHER KEVIN ALLEN DRAKES

CHAPTER
SEVEN

JORDAN NERVOUSLY PLAYED with his Army Ranger challenge coin, stuffed in his pants pocket with a bundle of zip-ties. He forced himself to stop and pulled his hood tighter. He was dressed in a black hoodie, camo cargo pants, and battered steel-toed boots from his old job as a dock worker.

He'd taken that job in his early twenties, working outside the union and getting paid under the table. It was good money, though nowhere near what dock workers officially made. He'd used the money to support himself while going to school. Orphans didn't have parents or relatives to house them or pay for college.

Jordan had always known he wanted to be a cop. He'd been rescued by a cop, a detective named Charles "Chuck" Benson. He was the first person who made Jordan actually feel worth something. He still talked to Chuck, though now retired. He was the closest thing to a father Jordan had, and the portraits of them fishing together hanging in his apartment were among Jordan's most valued treasures.

They were an odd juxtaposition, the two men, a black inner-city cop and an orphan from Russia. One white with blond hair and blue eyes, the other black as night with brown eyes and no hair. Jordan would have to visit Chuck and catch up. Maybe go fishing. That is, if he didn't get caught and arrested.

Jordan's smartwatch buzzed. He checked it. It was *another* call from Agent Kelly. He tapped the watch, sending the call to voicemail. She wouldn't like that, and he was sure he'd hear about it, if she left a voicemail that was anything like her last one:

"Griffin! This is your partner. You do know what that word means, right? Where are you? We have a backlog of cases a mile long, and LSPD keeps sending new requests. Call-me-back!"

He didn't have time for a new partner, or cold cases the police couldn't solve on their own. No, Jordan had a higher purpose, a holier purpose, and *that* was all that mattered.

Jordan stayed out several nights surveilling Evan Chandry's apartment, and knew the man's routine like a memorized poem:

Six o'clock, Evan arrives home from the office.

Six thirty, Evan works out in his apartment complex's gym.

Seven-forty, Evan takes a shower.

Eight o'clock, Evan makes himself dinner.

Eight-twenty, Evan watches TV and works on his laptop.

Ten-o'clock, Evan goes to bed.

Of course, there was some variation, and sometimes Evan would have friends over to play video games or watch sports. But that was largely the cadence of the man's life.

Not a man, a child killer, like Thanatos.

Jordan slipped out of the alley and melded with the crowd walking down the sidewalk. As he passed in front of Evan's apartment building, one of its tenants exited the front door, and Jordan caught it before it closed and locked. He glanced around before confidently striding in without bothering with the door code. He skipped the elevators and went straight for the stairwell, looking down to let his hood hide his face from the security cameras.

Evan lived eight flights up, and the jog up the stairs winded Jordan. He may be fit for duty, but having been forced to rest for several weeks had markedly brought down his physical endurance. He paused to catch his breath on the fifth floor. It would be a pathetic thing if his revenge mission was cut short because he couldn't run up a few flights of stairs.

Before he knew it, Jordan was ten again and climbing the decaying, wide steps of a grand staircase, its wooden banisters coated with thick dust. A little girl, no older than six, held his hand as he towed her up to the second floor. She was crying and clinging tightly to a naked Barbie doll with tangled hair. He could still hear the grating sound of the bone-saw. He'd tried to comfort her by telling her it was going to be okay. He had lied.

Jordan gritted his teeth, rage burning hot in his chest and giving his muscles new energy. He glanced up the stairwell and leapt into a run. When he reached the eighth floor, he paused, slipped on a pair of skin-tight, rubber gloves, and put his hands in his pockets before exiting the stairwell.

He walked down the hall, head down and unhurried, until he found Evan's apartment–number eight-twenty-three. He listened to make sure he was alone in the corridor before placing his left palm over the door-bell camera. With his right hand he fished a compact lockpick gun out of his pocket and inserted it into Evan's door-lock. With a quiet *click*, the lock gave and Jordan entered the man's apartment. He closed and locked the door behind him and turned to face the keypad set on the wall adjacent to the door. A red light to the side of the keys was blinking, and Jordan began mentally counting down from sixty.

He pressed and held the pound key for five seconds, then typed in zero-six-five-eight-nine–the security company's current override code. At least he hoped it was still the current one. That information had come from one of his more tech-savvy C.I.s and cost him more than a little cash to ensure the inquiry remained confidential.

The C.I. was a kid named Skylar and was by all outward appearances a loser, a high school dropout that worked at a gas station and lived with his parents. But Skylar was a technical genius and fed Jordan all kinds of info gleaned from the darknet.

Jordan held his breath.

The blinking red light turned green, and Jordan exhaled. The code had worked. He'd have to buy Skylar a drink sometime.

He took several steps into the room. It was much the same as the vacant unit he'd toured a few days earlier under a false identity. Jordan quickly found the Wi-Fi router and unplugged it to disable the apartment's cameras. Next, he found the box that recorded the camera footage and likewise disconnected it.

Jordan checked his watch. Evan would be back any minute. He moved into Evan's bedroom pulled another item from the pouch of his hoodie. A rubber mask–a skull mask.

Jordan put on the mask, but when he did, he found himself suddenly back at that place; that hell house, dragging an old travel trunk back down the dilapidated grand staircase.

His orders were to take it outside and cast it down the well. He had the nude Barbie in his free hand. Each thunk of the trunk crashing down on the stairs was like a knife in his little-boy heart. He gripped the old doll tightly, tears streaming down his face. After finally making it outside and hefting the trunk up onto the lip of the well, and then shoving it over and watching it disappear into the abyss, he picked up the doll. It was a pathetic thing, the paint of its right eye smudged and its hair short from an ill-advised haircut. He tossed it into the well. It belonged down there with her.

The sound of keys unlocking the front door brought Jordan back to the moment. He balled his fists and listened to the door swing open.

"Dad wants me at the rally Friday..." Evan said to someone.

Jordan froze. Was he not alone?

When no reply came but Evan continued talking, Jordan realized he was on his phone. Keys jangled as they were tossed onto a hard surface, probably a counter, and steps approached. Jordan quickly stepped toward the bedroom closet where he slid open one of the hanging doors and slipped inside, pulling the door shut just as the bedroom light ignited.

"No, I really don't have a choice, not as long as he pays my rent. He's turned into a hard ass since I got arrested."

Jordan balled his fists. This predator, this spoiled little child killer, was complaining about not having his freedom.

He shouldn't have any freedom. He should be in prison, or better yet, he should be dead!

"Yeah I'll text you later. Okay. Bye."

Jordan waited a beat to make sure Evan had disconnected the call, then flung open the door and rushed out. Evan released a startled scream and tried to stand from where he sat on his bed. He tripped and fell. Jordan crashed down on him, knees landing on his side. An audible crack reported a fractured rib, which made Jordan smile. Evan tried to cry out, but Jordan pounded his face until the young man was choking and sputtering on his own blood. The sound of his sobbing and the sight of his bloody face elicited absolutely no pity from Jordan.

Jordan stood, bent over, grabbed the young man by his hair, hauled him up, and tossed him onto the bed. Evan landed, saw his phone, and made a desperate move to grab it. Jordan leapt onto the bed, caught Evan's wrist, and wrenched it backward, snapping it. Jordan placed a gloved hand over Evan's mouth to muffle his scream. Unable to breathe through his broken and bloody nose, Evan started to thrash, and Jordan relented.

"Scream and my hand goes back over your mouth," Jordan growled. "And maybe it doesn't come off. Nod if you understand."

Evan nodded.

Jordan stood from the bed, grabbed Evan's phone, and placed it on a desk situated opposite from the foot of Evan's bed. Seeing through the skull mask wasn't easy, but Jordan had practiced moving around his apartment in the dark while wearing it, and his moves were confident and not the least bit clumsy. He was lucky Kate hadn't caught him. Some nights he'd practiced while she was sleeping, when his urge to drink was the strongest. The focus and thrill of it had dampened his thirst and became something of a pathological substitute.

Jordan pulled a bouquet of zip-ties from his pocket. He thought he heard something fall to the floor, but he didn't have time for phantom noises, not with a child killer to punish. Jordan presented the zip-ties, and Evan's eyes widened. He lunged away from Jordan, who quickly tackled the young man and forced him onto his stomach before binding his hands and feet.

"My dad is Senator Chandry," Evan choked out. "He has money."

That infuriated Jordan, and he punched Evan in the back of the head.

"Do you think that's what this is about?"

Evan didn't answer for a moment. Had Jordan hit him too hard? "What do you want?" he finally asked.

Jordan hopped off the bed and moved around so he was facing Evan, who lay on his stomach looking up at him. His eyes *were* unfocused.

I definitely hit him too hard.

Jordan didn't care how bad he hurt him, but he did want the monster conscious and to have his wits about him to fully appreciate what was coming.

"Why?" Evan croaked out.

"I'm here for Jorge Torres."

Evan stared, looking completely confused. "Who?"

Jordan ground his teeth. The piece of shit didn't even know the boy's name! He wanted so badly to fall on Evan and beat him until he stopped moving—stopped breathing—but he held to the promise he'd made to Kevin and, by extension, to God.

Jordan reached into his pocket and produced a paper that he unfolded and displayed to Evan. It was a black and white flyer with a picture of a little boy sporting a gap-tooth smile, and large block letters that read "M-I-S-S-I-N-G" printed above it.

"Jorge was the name of the five-year-old-boy you murdered."

Evan's sobbing intensified, which for Jordan, was confession enough. But he wanted others to know too. He turned back to the desk where he'd placed Evan's phone.

"What's the code?"

"What?" Evan sobbed.

"THE CODE!" barked Jordan.

"T...two, six, three, eight," stammered Evan.

Jordan's skintight rubber gloves allowed him to interact with the touch screen and he navigated to the recording app. "I want you to admit what you did to Jorge, including where you buried him, or I am going to slit your throat!"

Evan's eyes widened and he licked his lips.

Jordan took a step toward him.

"Okay, okay!" He cried harder, sniffling through his broken nose.

Jordan started the recording and held up the phone to Evan.

The disgusting piece of human misery that was Evan began detailing his murder of Jorge through sobs and intermittent pleas to God for forgiveness. There was a strange dichotomy to the young man that tempted Jordan to pity him, but Jordan wouldn't let go of his rage, and when those pangs of sorrow came he deliberately pictured the nearly bald Barbie doll held tight in the little girl's hand, and then the old trunk. Evan continued, and when Jordan thought he was obfuscating, he paused the recording to reiterate his threat, though empty, then resumed recording to allow Evan to elaborate the gruesome details of his kill.

Finally, he was finished, and Jordan stopped the recording. He saved it and scheduled it to send to all of Evan's contacts, including Senator Chandry, the next morning.

That should be enough time.

He put down the phone and walked over to Evan, who was crying again.

"You disgust me."

"I know. Please, I'm sick. I need help," Evan pled.

"No." Jordan pulled a rolled bandanna from his pocket. "You need justice."

Evan squeezed his eyes shut, hyperventilating. "Who are you?" he choked out.

Jordan stared at Evan a long moment before finally saying, "I'm Thanatos."

Before Evan could say more, Jordan shoved the rolled bandanna into his mouth. The man could barely breath through his nose, but after listening hard for a moment, Jordan decided he was getting enough air.

He went to the kitchen, pulled a large knife from the knife block, and froze.

He stared at the bloody butcher's knife. His fingers had cramped from holding it so tightly, he wasn't sure he could let go of it.

Jordan shook himself out of the memory and gripped the knife's handle hard. He returned to the bedroom where he found that Evan had rolled onto his back. His eyes widened when he saw the knife, and he tried to speak around the bandanna in his mouth.

"Don't worry," Jordan said. "As much as I may want to, I'm not going to kill you. I'm just going to make sure you don't hurt anyone else."

With that, Jordan rolled Evan back onto his stomach and used the knife to cut open the back of his shirt. This was the tricky part. He'd used Kate's knowledge as a trauma nurse—asking her detailed questions about the spine and where an injury would cause paralysis as opposed to death—to plan this part. When she asked why he was interested in spinal cord injuries, he simply told her it was for a case and he couldn't reveal details, which seemed to satisfy her.

He worried about finding the right spot, but fortunately, Evan was lean, and tracing his spine was easy. Jordan found what he believed was the location of the C-7 vertebrae and pressed the finger of his left hand down to mark the spot while he raised the knife with his right hand. If he did this wrong, he could kill Evan. His ambivalence at *that* thought disturbed him, and he momentarily faltered.

Evan strained at his bonds and tried to shout through the gag.

Jordan's nerves nearly failed him, and he lowered the knife. Then he remembered that pathetic, naked Barbie doll, and the fire in him reignited. He ground his teeth and gripped the handle of the knife tightly. Tears of anger rolled down his cheeks beneath the skull mask. He had as much killed that little girl as Evan had killed Jorge. But unlike Evan, he hadn't wanted to. His had been a crime of cowardice, whereas Evan's had been a crime of depravity, but that's where the difference ended. This was as much about paying for his sins as it was about punishing Evan's.

Jordan started cutting.

We had broken the laws of man, yes. But together, Agent Griffin and I had stopped a monster from taking the lives of more children, which I sincerely believe was the will of God.

JOURNAL OF FATHER KEVIN ALLEN DRAKES

CHAPTER
EIGHT

EDWARD ALEXANDER SLAMMED his right fist into Victor's jaw, followed by his left into Victor's stomach. He doubled over and Alexander's knee met his nose on the way down. Victor stumbled back, lost his balance, and fell onto the floor, where he stayed.

You can't hurt me, Edward. There's nothing you can do to me that hasn't already been done.

Faint laughter came from Uncle Simon.

"Do you realize what this will cost us, Victor?" Alexander asked, and his voice betrayed absolutely no anger, not even a bit of aggravation–just cold disappointment.

Victor started to rise, but a vicious kick to his ribs told him that had been premature.

"May I speak, sir?" Victor choked out.

Alexander kicked him twice more and then stomped on his back for good measure. "Yes."

Victor rolled onto his side, coughing violently. Alexander walked over to a plush leather executive chair positioned at a glass conference table and sat. He waved his bloody right hand and massaged it while waiting for Victor's coughing fit to pass.

Victor sat up, then stood, and limped over to face Alexander. He tossed Victor his pocket square and motioned at his own nose to indicate Victor should wipe the blood off *his* nose, which Victor did.

"You asked what this will cost?"

Alexander nodded and turned to stare through the wall of glass that was Axum Tower's east windows. It was night, and the cityscape was a horizon of shadows dotted with a constellation of lights.

"I imagine Escarra's Lieutenants have already pulled out of the deal, and their surrogates in Lake Side will cease all business transactions with us, if not becoming openly hostile."

Alexander glanced up at Victor and then back out the windows. "They blame us."

"As they should. It *was* our fault."

Alexander frowned, a subtle gesture, but one Victor recognized as a dangerous show of emotion for an otherwise very controlled man. "*Your* fault."

"Let me explain," Victor quickly added.

Alexander nodded.

"I have a theory about what happened this morning. I don't believe this was an attack on Escarra, or even an attack on your operation. I believe this was an attack on you, personally."

Alexander scoffed. "Poor planning then. I was never going to ride in that car."

"Not a physical attack. A calculated strike to stop you from expanding your operation, to make you look weak, and potentially create a powerful rival for you."

Alexander arched an eyebrow. "But why?"

Victor shook his head. "I think someone within your organization is trying to usurp you."

Alexander laughed. "No one would dare!"

Victor wiped blood from under his nostrils. "Something I'm sure Caesar thought."

Alexander stared at Victor for a long moment, and he half expected another round of beatings. "You have balls, Victor," Alexander finally said. "That's part of why I like you. I'll float this idea with my people."

"And if one of them is in on it?"

"Careful not to overstep, Victor."

Victor knelt–*David's suggestion*–and bowed his head. "Sir, you are correct that this is *my* fault. I am charged with your safety and the safety of your guests. Despite whoever else was involved in the logistics, I bore ultimate responsibility for Escarra's safety. Please, let me investigate this. Let me redeem myself."

Alexander let him stay like that, on his knees in silent discomfort, for what felt like five minutes, but when Victor risked a glance at his watch, it was only two.

"Get up," Alexander ordered.

Victor stood.

"In my experience, only two kinds of people have ever professed this kind of dog-like devotion to me: self-aggrandizing fools, and true loyalists."

"And which am I?" Victor asked.

"Honestly?" Alexander rubbed his temples. "I don't know, yet. I obviously trust you with my safety or we wouldn't meet alone like this. But I also know you're dangerous, which is why you're my bodyguard and chief enforcer. However, tonight you showed me you're much more dangerous than I realized, because tonight you revealed you're also a lot smarter than I gave you credit for."

"Not smart enough to detect the plot to kill Escarra," Victor said.

Alexander's eyes narrowed. "Don't do that. There are few things I hate more than false modesty, Victor. Even intelligent men make mistakes."

Victor nodded. That had been a misstep. He needed to be more careful.

Alexander sighed. "I am going to give you the benefit of the doubt. You're young, and I think your ridiculous display here meant to show loyalty can be chalked up to that. I tend to think you are loyal and that your heart is in the right place. I will allow you to prove it by investigating Escarra's assassination. Find out who killed him, and you will have my forgiveness. Just don't let your pet theory about a usurper blind you. Follow the evidence and find who was responsible. I want them to confess to me, and then I will kill them. Understand?"

"Yes, sir," Victor said.

Alexander waved him away.

Victor turned and began lurching with as much dignity as he could toward the room's glass double doors.

"Oh, and Victor?"

Victor stopped and turned back. "Yes, Mr. Alexander?"

"If you don't find who's responsible, I will hold *you* responsible. And you know what that means."

"I do, sir."

VICTOR WINCED as he pressed an icepack to his ribs. He sat on the leather sofa in his penthouse, leaning back so the second icepack balanced on his face wouldn't fall off while he nursed his ribs, all for a modicum of relief. Dark purple splotches decorated his naked torso, as well as his face. It was not lost on him that he very well could have died tonight.

That man couldn't kill you, Uncle Simon said. *You're ten times the killer he is.*

Victor ignored the voice.

David was livid when he saw his condition, Victor had to talk his best friend out of going to Alexander's office to avenge him. That made him smile, which evoked a groan of pain. David was a good man—his brother in all but blood.

Their plan, while not perfect, was working. Now Victor had to create an enemy within Alexander's own inner circle. He wasn't sure what kind of timeline he was on, but as long as he could demonstrate he was making regular progress in his investigation, that should keep Alexander from executing him, for a while at least.

A chime from the wall-mounted intercom tore Victor from his reverie. "Mr. Reese, you have a guest."

Victor checked his watch. It was late. The only ones who ever visited him this late were David and Dawson, and he'd already met with both. He groaned again as he forced himself off the coach, both his icepacks falling to the leather cushions. He cradled his ribs as he made his way to the screen on the wall and pressed the button. An image appeared of a Latina woman with chin length hair. She was dressed in a sweater and jeans, and this time she was wearing sunglasses, but there was no mistaking her for anyone else–it was Camilla, Escarra's bodyguard.

Victor's mouth became an arid desert. "Send her up."

His heart pounded, and Victor wasn't sure if it was from fear or excitement. The adrenaline muted his pain, and he snatched up his .45 from off the sofa. Had she figured out he was behind the car bombing that killed her *Papi*? Was she here to exact vengeance?

The elevator chimed, and the doors started to open. Victor put the gun behind his back and clicked off the safety as he spun to face the elevator. The doors fully opened, and Camilla stepped out of the elevator and into the penthouse.

"Victor–" She stopped. She took off her sunglasses and stared at him. "What happened to you?"

"Mr. Alexander was not happy with me for what happened to Mr. Escarra. I'm lucky to be alive, really. To what do I owe the pleasure, Camilla?"

Camilla glanced at Victor's right side where his arm was hidden behind his back. "I come unarmed."

She raised her hands so her sweater pulled up to show off her toned, brown midriff and did a parody of a fashion twirl. She indeed had no guns in her waistband. Victor swallowed. She was very beautiful.

"I just came to thank you for saving my life."

"I apologize." Victor brought his arm back out in front of him, clicked the safety back on his .45, and walked it over to a side table where he deposited it. He expected a reprimand from Uncle Simon, but nothing came. He was starting to notice a pattern. When he was in Camilla's presence, his uncle was either muted or gone entirely. That was a significant relief, a quiet reprieve in the sea of deafening chaos his mind was becoming.

"I don't get many late-night visitors."

"Not even the ladies?" Camilla smirked. "No woman?"

Victor laughed, surprised to find it was genuine. "Not particularly interested in women."

Camilla looked embarrassed. "Oh. I... I didn't realize. So, you're..."

It dawned on Victor just what his answer had sounded like, and he quickly jumped in. "No, no, no. That's not what I meant. I'm not."

"It's ok," Camilla said. "I don't judge."

The situation was spinning completely out of his control, something he wasn't used to at all. He didn't like that. "Camilla, I am not gay. I've had women, just not a girlfriend. What we do is different. It's so dangerous and ugly, I can't see sharing it with a romantic partner."

Camilla looked relieved. "So, none of your men have wives or girl-friends?"

Victor thought of David and Anne. He expected Uncle Simon to comment on how Anne wasn't her real name, but again, he was gone.

"Well, some do. But..." Victor nodded, and a sharp pain shot through his face making him gasp.

Camilla immediately closed the distance between them and examined the ugly bruises on his face. She reached up to touch him, and he flinched.

"I'm not going to hurt you."

Victor nodded and let Camilla examine him. She pressed gently on his bruises, and his jaw tightened as he weathered the pain. A wave of exhilaration washed over him as she moved in so close he could smell her scent, a pleasant mix of shampoo and perfume.

"Good news, I don't think anything on your face is broken." She lightly traced her fingers down his neck, lingering a little before moving over his chest and to his left side. It was very sensual and mildly arous-ing... until Camilla pressed in hard with two fingers.

"Dammit!" Victor shouted and jerked away.

Camilla smirked. "Your ribs are a different story—definitely broken. I'm going to need to wrap them." She walked past him and headed toward the bedroom. "Where's your bathroom?"

Victor was too stunned to stop her. "Hey!"

Camilla opened his bedroom door, took a few steps in, and stopped. "What happened to the mirror?"

Victor caught up to her and grabbed her by the forearm. She looked up at him, and for the first time, he registered fear in her face.

Camilla wrenched her arm free and took as step away. "Why?"

"Why what?"

"Why did you save me?"

Victor clenched his jaw. The truth was, he didn't know why. He wasn't supposed to have done that. In fact, if he was smart, he would kill her now to tidy up the loose end he'd created.

"How did you know the car was going to blow?" Camilla persisted.

That's why she really came.

Victor didn't answer.

"It was you," Camilla said softly.

Victor closed his eyes. Now he had no choice.

Warm, moist lips suddenly pressed against his, Camilla pulling his head down so their faces could meet. He pulled away.

"Thank you," Camilla gushed through tears.

"Thank you?"

Camilla wiped her eyes. "For sending that *hijo de puta* to hell!"

Now Victor *was* confused. "You're happy Escarra is dead?"

Camilla's eyes shifted so she was looking sideways, not meeting his gaze. "He didn't just call me his daughter; I *was* his daughter–all his female attendants are. And we weren't just his help, we were also his harem, and none of it by choice." She looked back at Victor. "So yes, I'm very, *very* happy that you blew that incestuous *cabron* to pieces. You set me free, Victor."

She's not so different from me. A slave to a horribly abusive relative.

Victor stared at her for a long moment.

She waited for him to react, not looking like the toned and dangerous femme fatale he'd originally made her out to be, but a vulnerable, emotionally fragile creature who surprisingly shared a piece of his own tattered soul.

Victor leaned in and passionately kissed her, ignoring the pain as the two moved into his bedroom and toward his bed. They fell onto the bed and paused their kissing so Camilla could remove her top.

Victor smiled at seeing Camilla's bra was custom designed to hold a small pistol between the breasts. "You said you were unarmed."

Camilla smirked and let Victor remove the gun.

He expected Uncle Simon to comment on how he should dispose of her when he was finished deriving pleasure from her, but the taunting voice never came.

But what I hadn't known when Agent Griffin and I made our first compact, was that I was playing with fire. Jordan is not well. He is a good man, and I believe at his core he is a hero, but within him rages a terrible tempest of guilt and wrath.

JOURNAL OF FATHER KEVIN ALLEN DRAKES

CHAPTER
NINE

CRYING DRIFTED up from the dilapidated well…

"Jordan," the little girl called. "Jordan…"

"Jordan!"

Jordan woke to Kate nudging him. He was curled up on their living room sofa wearing only his boxers. He'd bundled his bloody clothing, packed them in a plastic garbage bag, and stowed it under the seat in his Jeep. He'd burn them in their firepit later when Kate wasn't around.

"What?" Jordan rubbed his eyes.

Kate was still dressed in her scrubs. She must've just walked in the door. "It's nine. Don't you have a morning briefing?"

Jordan's eyes flew open. "Shit!"

He stood and made for the bedroom, but Kate caught him by the hand. "What's this?"

The focus of her attention was a gash across the top of his left hand where he'd cut himself when the knife he was using to sever Evan Chandry's spinal cord had slipped.

He wrenched his hand out of hers. "It's nothing."

Kate frowned. "Was it a bar fight?"

"No!"

Jordan rushed up the stairs and Kate followed him. He flew into the bedroom and slid aside the closet door, indiscriminately pulling a dress shirt from its hanger and threading his arm into it.

"I was thinking," Kate began, her tone suddenly devoid of irritation, "since you're already late, why don't you just take a sick day?"

Jordan scoffed. "What?"

"I'm serious," Kate said. "You can play hooky, and we can spend the day together."

Having finished buttoning up his shirt, Jordan slipped on his suit pants. "You just got off a shift. Don't you want to sleep?"

Kate flashed a wicked smile. "Well, I was thinking we could both spend part of the day in bed."

Jordan quickly donned a matching suit jacket. "I'm sorry, honey. It sounds really nice, but I can't."

Kate's smile faded, and she just stared at him.

Jordan strapped on his holster and gun before giving Kate a quick peck on the cheek and rushing downstairs with a tie in one hand and shoes in the other.

The look of hurt on his wife's face was not lost on him, Jordan just pretended he didn't see it.

"Well, look who decided to grace us with his presence," ASAC Seigers said when Jordan slipped into the conference room.

"I'm sorry for being late." Jordan found an empty seat at the glass conference room table, one that was deliberately several chairs away from Agent Kelly who was desperately trying to catch his attention.

Seigers rolled his eyes and returned to his slide presentation.

Jordan flexed his right hand underneath the conference table. He hadn't realized wedging a knife between two vertebrae and cutting through sinew would leave him so sore. He rubbed a pair of old scars on his right hand, scars he couldn't remember getting no matter how hard he racked his brain. Ironically, they matched his new wound.

When rubbing his joints failed to alleviate the pain, Jordan stuck his hand in his pocket and searched for his challenge coin, but it wasn't there.

Must've left it in my other pants. He was surprised at himself. He'd never forgotten the good luck charm before, but he *had* rushed out of the house.

Now that the adrenaline rush of being late had worn off, Jordan's late night was starting to haunt him. He nursed a tepid cup of coffee to stave off the drowsiness. Seigers kept shooting him dirty looks as he droned on about several cold cases they were assigned to help the local police solve.

Jordan started to drift.

He was in Thanatos's science room with the special table that had all the straps. There was a bone saw on another table and a bucket under the table filled with urine and excrement.

"I'm sorry, but what is it about the rape and decapitation of two young college co-eds that you find boring, Agent Griffin?"

Jordan started at Seigers' voice, knocking over his coffee.

Everyone in the room stared at him.

Jordan ground his teeth. Seigers was an ass. Since their confrontation in Tom's office, Seigers had been busting his balls every chance the chubby man got.

Jordan scrambled to wipe up the coffee with napkins leftover from an order of bagels someone brought to the morning briefing. "I'm sorry. I had a late night."

"So did half the people in this room, but you don't see us falling asleep in our coffee. Keep your damn eyes open, got it?"

Jordan clenched his jaw. "Yes, sir."

After several more agonizing, cloudy minutes–probably only ten if Jordan was being honest–the morning briefing was over. He was starting to doze again when he was jolted back to full wakefulness by the sound of dozens of overlapping conversations mixed with the footsteps of those leaving.

"Agent Griffin." A woman tapped him on the shoulder.

Jordan looked up to find Agent Kelly standing over him, dressed in another immaculate pant suit—hair, nails and makeup as perfect as any social media influencer.

"Agent Kelly." Jordan made to take a sip of his coffee only to find the Styrofoam cup empty.

"You haven't been returning my calls."

Jordan scratched the side of his head. "I know. I've not felt well."

Kelly arched an eyebrow. "Too sick to text?"

He shrugged.

Kelly rolled her eyes. "You see this?" She presented her phone to him. On it was a news story.

Jordan squinted. It was about Evan Chandry. Fear stabbed Jordan in the chest, but he smothered his reaction. "No. What's it about?"

Agent Kelly turned the phone back to herself and scrolled through the text. "Senator Chandry's son—Evan—was attacked in his apartment last night. It was nasty too. The attacker apparently severed Evan's spinal cord."

"Ouch." Jordan folded his laptop and slipped it into his messenger bag. "Probably killed him to get back at the senator for something."

That sounded convincing, right?

"No, that's where this gets weird."

Jordan collected a notepad and pen from the table, put them in his bag, and closed it.

"Evan was definitely the target, and he's not dead."

Jordan looked up at Kelly, doing his best not to betray anything. "Okay, you've got my full attention."

Kelly sat in the empty seat next to Jordan, smiling and acting way too excited to be talking about a violent crime.

"So, get this! Someone attacks Evan in his apartment, binds him, cuts his spine so he'll be a quadriplegic the rest of his life, but before he does that, he makes him record a confession!"

Jordan's heart was racing. He didn't trust himself to speak, but knew he had to. "What did he confess?"

Kelly leaned in as though sharing a secret. "To murdering a five-year-old boy named Jorge Torres!"

Jordan had to work to control his breathing. "Is it true?"

Kelly leaned back. "Lake Side Homicide is investigating the area where Evan said he buried the body. We'll know soon enough."

A horrifying thought occurred to Jordan. What if Kelly suspected him?

He spoke before he had the chance to think better of it. "Why are you telling me this?"

Kelly smiled. "SAC Morrison *told* me you were smart. Yes, there is a reason I'm telling you this." She returned to scrolling on her phone until she found something in the text. "There." She showed Jordan the article.

Jordan squinted, but he couldn't see anything standing out from the article. He shook his head. "I don't get it."

Kelly turned the phone back to herself and read aloud. "An anonymous source inside LSPD told the paper that while Chandry wasn't lucid enough to give a statement, he was heard repeating the following: 'I'm sick, God forgive me, and Thanatos'."

Jordan froze. Not just his movements, every part of him became rigid as though he'd turned to ice. Why had he been so stupid? "Thanatos?"

"Yeah!" Kelly grinned. "That can't be a coincidence, right?"

"Anyone who has a superficial knowledge of Greek mythology, hell, even modern psychology, could know that name." Jordan stood.

Kelly's grin faded. "You're not even the least bit curious?"

"Leave it alone, Kelly. Thanatos is dead." Jordan started walking toward the conference room door.

Kelly stood. "How do you know that? No one ever figured out who he was."

Jordan squeezed his eyes shut. Dammit, he shouldn't have said that. He was making too many mistakes today. Must be the sleep deprivation.

"How else do you explain his disappearance?" He left the conference room before Kelly could respond.

Jordan made his way out of the office and down to the parking garage where he found his Jeep. He sat in the driver's seat for an indeterminable amount of time, lost in thought and memory, remembering the details of what he'd done to Evan, and working to reassure himself that it had been right. He couldn't quite get there. Something nagged at him, an irrepressible patch of icy guilt. It was ridiculous. The man was a child molester and murderer. If anything, Jordan hadn't gone far enough. In the heat of the moment, during the haze of righteous anger, it had felt right, but now…

Jordan started his Jeep and pulled out of the garage. He was supposed to be in a meeting with Kelly and local detectives working on several cold cases, but that was futile. He needed to talk to Kevin Drakes.

He ignored and broke several traffic laws on his way to the cathedral but made it there without getting pulled over. Jordan jogged up the steps, slipped in the doors, and ignored another priest's offer of assistance as he scanned the pews. He spotted Kevin sitting near the front, chatting with the young homeless man he'd seen the last time he'd been here. Jordan rushed down the center aisle, catching Kevin's eyes as the priest looked up at his approach.

"Jordan," Kevin greeted him politely, but Jordan caught the irritation in the priest's normally affable tone.

"I need to talk to you."

"I'm with another parishioner at the moment. Please wait over there." Kevin motioned to a pew on the other side of the aisle.

Jordan opened his mouth to object, but Kevin cut him off with a very firm, "Please."

Jordan glanced at the disheveled young man the priest was ministering to, then stalked off to sit and wait. He drew in a deep breath and stared up above the altar at the large statue of Jesus of Nazareth with arms extended as he hung on the cross, a crown of thorns digging into his brow, his bearded face grimacing in pain. Jordan glanced at Kevin and his parishioner, then back up at the statue. Though it was only inanimate marble, he found he couldn't meet the statue's eyes.

He was ashamed of what he'd done to Evan, to one of the Good Shepherd's flock, lost and diseased though that sheep was. That shame was short lived as Jordan's thoughts shifted to the things Evan had confessed to, and his guilt was consumed in a rising flame of fierce anger. He snapped his head back up, casting a gaze at the statue that was no longer adoring but accusing.

I don't feel guilty, and I don't need your forgiveness! Evan got less than he deserved, and I stopped a monster from hurting more innocent children! I did what you didn't do for me! Where were you when I needed you? Why did you let him take me?

He half expected some sign of God's anger toward him, but nothing happened. He glanced over at Kevin and found him still talking with the young, homeless man.

Kyle, Kevin had said his name was.

Kevin gripped his shoulder, smiled, then stood. Kyle nodded, stood, and shook Kevin's hand before turning and striding up the aisle between the pews. Jordan watched the young man leave as soft footfalls told him Kevin was approaching. The priest sat next to him on the pew.

"Kyle right?" Jordan asked.

"You have a good memory," Kevin said. "You and Kyle have a lot in common, actually; He's a veteran with PTSD, and some tragedies in his past, struggling with substance abuse."

"You don't know me," Jordan snapped.

Kevin sighed. "I know tortured souls when I see them."

Ignoring that, Jordan glanced around to make sure no one was in earshot, then said in a low tone, "I took care of Evan."

Kevin frowned and answered in a hushed tone, "Yes. I read about it. Thank you for keeping your promises."

Jordan gave Kevin a curt nod.

"Well, since the deed is done, if you want to follow me to the confessional, I can absolve you of your sin, and we can put this ugly business behind us." Kevin stood.

Jordan grabbed Kevin's sleeve. "I need another name."

Kevin wrenched his arm out of Jordan's grasp. "What?"

The priest standing near the entrance cleared his throat, and both Jordan and Kevin glanced at him.

Kevin waved a hand. "It's all right, Hector."

Jordan stood and leaned in close to Kevin. "I need you to give me the name of another offender."

"That wasn't the deal," Kevin whispered.

"Please, I need this."

Kevin glanced around and then motioned for Jordan to follow him. He led Jordan out of the sanctuary, into a side corridor, and then into what appeared to be a kind of storage room for file cabinets.

Jordan's pulse quickened with anticipation. He was going to get another target, someone else he could make suffer for their sins. Another chance to strike back, to turn the darkness on itself, to make Thanatos pay. The thrill was better than chasing any drink, it was even better than the sultry promise of sex.

Kevin closed the door behind them, and then rounded on him. "What is wrong with you? Do you realize how unhinged you sound?"

Kevin's words were like a cold slap across Jordan's face. Until now the sagely priest had been affable and restrained even when it came to grim matters. But now, Kevin was angry, and he wasn't holding back.

"I...I..." Jordan stammered.

"Our agreement was for *one* name." Kevin held up his index finger. "God help me, that alone was way out of line, and we should both go to prison for it, but it had to be done! Now you want to do it again. Why?"

"Because we actually made a difference."

"Do you think I'm an idiot?" Kevin snapped. "I take confessions for a living; I know a lie when I hear one!"

"Kevin, I need to do this!"

"You *need*?" Kevin threw up his hands. "Do you know what you sound like?"

Jordan balled his fists. "Why don't you tell me?"

"A dipsomaniac jonesing for a drink!"

Jonesing for a drink.

The words stung. Jordan hadn't had a drop of alcohol since he started his mission to bring *justice* to Evan. Had he just traded one addiction for another?

"What's this really about, Jordan? Why are you so hellbent on torturing deviants?"

Jordan's anger drained away, and he collapsed onto a wooden stool set next to one of the filing cabinets. "I've never told anybody, not my closest friends, not Kate, not even Chuck, of all people." Jordan laughed.

"Who's Chuck?" Kevin asked.

"He found me walking a forest road in the middle of the night. My feet were bloody, and I don't remember where the house was. I've actually gone looking for it several times."

"Jordan, what are you talking about? What is it that you never told anybody?"

Jordan swallowed and held his breath a moment to stop the tears. "My name."

Kevin shook his head. "I don't understand."

"Jordan Griffin was the name given to me by my first set of foster parents, the Griffins. But they couldn't handle me. I was too broken and too angry. So I went back into the system, the first of many times—in and out, in and out. If it hadn't been for Chuck... He was always there, the only stable thing in my life. The only one who cared. I wish he could've adopted me, but his personal life was kind of a mess."

It was all tumbling out in a jumbled heap. After decades it was all coming unraveled, and he was breaking down. It was too heavy to carry alone anymore.

"What is your real name?" Kevin gently asked.

"I only remember my first name—Yuri."

"Like Jorge," Kevin softly said.

Jordan nodded. "Both are George in English, and my family were immigrants too, so yeah, I guess when you told me about his abduction and murder it kind of hit close to home." He wiped his eyes. "The last time I saw my family I was ten. I still remember bits and pieces of the language, so I know my family was from Russia, or at least a Russian speaking country, but I only remember living here, so we must've come when I was younger.

"I do remember we were poor, like really poor. Papa worked a menial job, I'm not sure exactly what it was but I remember him wearing a blue worker's jumpsuit, like a maintenance worker or mechanic or something. Mama stayed home with me and my older sister–we didn't go to public school for some reason. Looking back on it, we were very secretive. We didn't socialize much and kept to ourselves. I think we might've been in the country illegally."

Kevin closed the distance between them and placed a hand on Jordan's shoulder. "Jordan, tell me what happened?"

Jordan met Kevin's eyes. "He killed them."

"Your family was murdered?"

Jordan stared down at the sickly green shag carpet, likely installed before he was born. Why hadn't it ever been replaced?

"He broke into our apartment at night. I didn't actually see or hear him kill my parents or sister. I just remember that when he came for me, his scythe was dripping blood."

"Scythe?"

Jordan nodded. "He was also wearing a skull mask."

Kevin's eyes widened and he crossed himself. "Your family was murdered by The Mad Reaper?"

"He called himself Thanatos."

"The Greek god of death?"

"Yeah," Jordan said. "He worshipped death."

"But he didn't kill *you*."

This is where Jordan's part in the story shifted from victim to villain. He bowed his head again, swallowed hard, and found he couldn't speak.

A full minute passed, prompting Kevin to nudge him. "Jordan?"

When Jordan finally answered, his voice was low and husky. "I helped him, Kevin."

"Helped him? You were a child…"

"Exactly!" Jordan stood so fast that Kevin nearly fell as he stepped back. "I helped him lure a little girl into his car! That was my job, to lure victims for him."

Kevin's face paled and he crossed himself.

Heat and pressure rose inside Jordan, like every part of him was going to burst into flame and detonate in a nuclear blast. "There were dozens I lured for him, but the one I remember is the little girl. I found her at a playground. She was by herself, sitting on a swing, and she was so friendly. She showed me her Barbie doll and told me its name. Then she asked me to push her on the swing, which I did for almost an hour. I wanted to tell her to run, but he was watching from his car. She came with me so willingly, because she trusted me. She had no idea I was leading her to her death, and the worst part is, I don't even remember her name!" Jordan scooped up the wooden stool and slammed it repeatedly against the nearest file cabinet, shattering it into its component pieces and then some.

Kevin winced with each impact, but to his credit, he didn't run or call for help.

Jordan dropped the broken stool and pounded on one of file cabinets, leaving dents in the beige aluminum top.

"I dropped a trunk with her corpse in it down a well!" Jordan pushed one of the cabinets over.

He slumped to the floor, sitting so his back was to Kevin, and gripped the hair on the top of his head as he sobbed and folded in on himself.

Kevin sunk down beside him, fussing with the bottom of his cassock as he folded his legs beneath him. Jordan expected him to quote scripture or tell him that he'd been just a child when he lured the little girl into the clutches of the greatest evil to ever stalk the streets of their city, and that it wasn't something he needed to feel guilty over. He'd tried that one on himself. It didn't work.

Instead, Kevin remained quiet.

They sat like that for a long time.

The priest was the one to finally break the silence. "Harold Jameson."

"What?" Jordan wiped his nose on his sleeve.

"He and his wife own a chain of daycares that cater to low-income single mothers. She runs them, but he's been using his access to make and distribute child pornography. They're not super wealthy, but they're well-connected, and given the limited resources of their clientele, they've managed to escape the consequences of a handful of accusations. I don't think the wife is involved, so please don't hurt her. And before you ask, I came by this information through the confession of one of Harold's customers, a man who'd purchased videos from him. He hadn't actually touched any children, and I'm seeing to it that he's getting help."

"Why are you giving me another name?"

Kevin drew in a deep breath. "Do you believe in God, Jordan?"

Jordan hesitated. One of his foster families had been Methodist, and he'd gone to church regularly until he was an older teen. Despite his lack of attendance, he'd never renounced his faith, and he *did* pray–though he didn't know where he stood with the Lord, as evidenced by his conversation with Him a few minutes earlier. "Yeah."

"Then you have to see some purpose in this." Kevin motioned around the room.

"In what?"

"In our meeting. In what we've done to save lives. In what we could accomplish together. In my being a priest, someone who can help you."

Jordan was about to say he didn't need help, but the sight of the overturned filing cabinet and the broken stool gave the lie to that statement. "How can *you* help *me*?"

"Well," Kevin raised his eyebrows and shrugged, "For starters, I have a master's degree in psychology. I'm also kind of a servant of the Almighty."

Jordan didn't know how to respond. His life was spiraling out of control. He and Kate barely spoke anymore, and though he didn't want to, he just kept pushing her away. Likely she thought he was drowning in alcohol. But the truth was much worse. His past, what he'd worked so hard to repress and keep at bay, was reaching out of the shadows of memory to destroy him, and he was much farther gone than he'd realized. He was losing his mind. Everything was on the line, and he was trapped.

Maybe God *had* sent him Kevin.

"This is what I propose," Kevin said. "We meet regularly, and you share everything with me about what happened to you when you were a child so I can help you work through it. In return, I will supply names of offenders who require an extralegal intervention to prevent them from harming additional victims—no revenge hits. Same rules as the Evan case apply, though, meaning you can't kill anyone."

Kevin's tone softened. "Jordan, this vigilante thing isn't going to save you. It's just a temporary fix, like your drinking. You have to face what happened to you, what you've done, and find a constructive way to move past it. I can help you do that. Will you let me help you? Will you let God help you?"

Jordan stared at Kevin for a long moment before nodding.

Kevin smiled and put his arm around him. Jordan leaned forward, shoulders shaking as he sobbed harder than he'd ever sobbed before.

When Jordan had regained some emotional control he asked, "Why?"

"Why what?"

"Why did God let The Mad Reaper kill my family? We prayed, Kevin. Mama read us the Bible. We were good people. We didn't hurt anyone. Why did God let Thanatos take me?"

Kevin sighed. "I don't know. All I know is that God had a reason."

"A reason for letting Thanatos use me to commit horrors?"

Kevin pulled his arm back and folded his hands in his lap. "People don't like this answer, but the truth is, God has his reasons for allowing the awful things in life to occur, and he doesn't usually explain those reasons to us because frankly, we aren't equipped to understand. It'd be a bit like a university professor trying to explain quantum mechanics to a toddler."

"That's a cop out."

"From me or God?" Kevin laughed.

Jordan didn't answer. He wasn't in the mood for one of Kevin's light-hearted sermons.

"Look, if it helps, I believe God wouldn't have asked this of you if he didn't intend to someday reveal why. And when that time comes, you'll understand God's reasons."

"We'll see," Jordan muttered.

Kevin groaned as he stood up. "Now, time to put those crime fighting muscles of yours to work and help me clean up this mess."

Jordan looked up at him.

"What? You didn't think you'd get to have an explosive emotional breakdown in my file room and not have to clean it up, did you?"

With my decision to help Jordan, I felt as though something in my future locked into place, that before, I was at a crossroads, and then my course was set and there was no going back. I fear the dream I had was more than a mere dream.

JOURNAL OF FATHER KEVIN ALLEN DRAKES

CHAPTER
TEN

THE RESTAURANT, really a restaurant by day and a bar by night, was little more than a hole in the wall that was part of a crumbling boardwalk on Lake Side's less affluent south side, but it was a safe place to talk. Their chicken masala also wasn't half bad, so Victor invested in the place, making sure the owner and his staff were loyal to him.

They sat in a booth with worn, cracking leather seats, Victor and Camilla on one side, both dressed in jeans and T-shirts, and David sitting opposite. He was dressed a little more formally—slacks, blazer, and a button-down shirt. Victor remembered when his best friend and adopted brother was an orphan dressed in oversized, thread-bare clothes that weren't fit for donation. Now David preferred high fashion and the finer things. That made Victor smile. His smile faded as he braced himself for

Uncle Simon's criticism, but it didn't come. He hadn't heard the lunatic since the night Camilla had come to his penthouse. The mental silence wasn't unwelcome, it was just... different.

Victor had heard his uncle's taunting critical voice for so long—decades actually–ever since the man had died. At first he'd really thought it was Uncle Simon's ghost haunting him. He'd never told anyone about it. Well, no one except Jenny.

Not Jenny, Anne.

He had to work hard to remember to refer to her by her new identity even all these years later.

She'd seemed concerned when he told her he heard their uncle's voice, but she didn't think it was anything supernatural. She did tell him not tell anyone else, especially the sisters or the priest, and definitely not the doctors. If he did, they might separate them. Victor kept that counsel and learned to deal with Uncle Simon's voice by reciting catechisms he'd learned from the sisters, thinking it would ward off his uncle's evil spirit. But as he grew older, he realized he wasn't dealing with a ghost, or so he thought until he'd actually seen Uncle Simon a few nights earlier.

Then Camilla came, and where scripture had failed, her influence succeeded. Uncle Simon was gone, exorcised by her attentions and maybe... her love? He wasn't sure. He wasn't sure he'd know love if he encountered it. He'd had girlfriends before, but it'd always been superficial, based on physical attraction that didn't last longer than a few months. And as Victor climbed the ranks of Alexander's syndicate, those kinds of relationships had had to stop, and he'd eventually settled for flings and trysts only to satisfy his needs. But Camilla, she was unlike any woman he'd ever met. She thrilled him, she enticed him, she confused him, and he loved it.

Camilla sat next to him playing with a small knife. It was one of a set she carried, a custom design with the image of a rose with a thorny stem engraved on the silver handle. It was beautiful and dangerous, like Camilla herself.

As he admired her, Victor became aware of David's stare. He cleared his throat and looked up at his friend. Indeed, he was staring, his face an ebony mask of disapproval.

"Did you hear about Senator Chandry's son?" Victor asked him.

David poked an ice cube in his glass of water. "Some maniac broke into his apartment and made him into a quadriplegic."

"Right. Well one of our people in the D.A's office passed along that the assailant was wearing a skull mask and called himself Thanatos."

David looked up at him. "What does *that* mean?"

Victor shook his head. "Not sure, but the assailant forced Evan Chandry to confess to murdering a child, and now Senator Chandry is useless to Edward, and he's irritated. Will you look into it for us?"

"Yeah."

"What is Thanatos?" Camilla asked.

Victor was about to answer when Dawson arrived, hair its typical brown mess and his face covered in a patchwork of whiskers that wasn't quite a beard. He wore what he always wore; reflective sunglasses, and a ratty trench coat over an unwashed second-hand T-shirt and jeans. He looked homeless. Victor told everyone he preferred Dawson to dress like that because it gave him a tactical advantage, allowing him to blend in and strike from anonymity, but that was only partially true. Victor knew the truth: Dawson was a mad dog that only he could keep leashed, so long as Victor provided him his regular allotment of explosives, opportunities for violence, and a steady stream of disposable prostitutes.

Dawson dropped a manilla envelope on the table before plopping down next to David. David glowered at Dawson, and Victor pictured a wolf growling a warning at a jackal.

"Randy said it's all there," Dawson said, completely oblivious to David's visible annoyance. "License, passport, birth certificate. Everything she needs to be Rosa Rojas."

Camilla shot a glance at Victor. "Red rose? Really?"

Victor laughed and put up his hands. "I didn't choose the name! I warned you Randy has a weird sense of humor."

"No one is going to believe that's my name."

"Just blame it on your parents." Victor grabbed the envelope and opened it, sorting through and examining the documents. "Besides, it's just temporary."

Camilla looked at Victor, smiled, and the two kissed.

"Why don't we get down to business?" David cut in.

Victor broke the kiss and looked at his friend. Camilla smirked at David and made to kiss Victor again, but he avoided it.

Victor shared a long look with David. He wasn't taking this well, which was a bit confusing as he was always telling Victor that he needed a woman in his life.

"No, David's right. This is important. I'm on a deadline—literally." He chuckled.

David's annoyed glower flickered, and he glanced at Camilla before looking back at Victor. "What're you talking about?"

"I don't have an exact date, but the clock *is* ticking. If I don't produce a believable culprit for the bombing that killed Escarra, Edward is going to kill me."

David's jaw tightened. "You failed to mention that."

"I'm telling you now," Victor snapped.

Camilla raised a soothing hand. "It's okay, David. We will think of a plan."

"*We* had a plan." David motioned at Victor and himself. "I don't know *you*."

Victor caught a grin from Dawson. Apparently he was enjoying the drama, or he was ogling Camilla. Victor made a mental note to remember not to leave Camilla alone with him.

"That *plan* we had has gone to hell!" Victor pounded a fist on the table, rattling the glasses and making everyone jump–everyone except Dawson. "We no longer have time to play the long game. We have to move quickly and present a threat to Edward now! Once we've created a believable enemy within his own ranks, I'll propose he consolidate the enforcers under one head—me. He'll see it as an ambitious move on my part instead of his own idea as we originally wanted, but he respects power plays like that. All we need to do is decide on a candidate and a path forward."

David seethed, not replying but instead choosing to stare at the table.

Victor stared at his friend for a long time and then glanced at Dawson, who just shrugged and started digging for something inside his trench coat.

Victor nodded. "Okay, I'll take that for consensus. Now, our candidate has to be someone Edward will genuinely believe is working against him."

"What about Jackson Banks?" Dawson said, a cigarette dangling from his lips as he tried to light it with a silver zippo lighter, one apparently low on fuel. Victor could guess why it was low–Dawson being a self-professed pyromaniac and there having been a string of arsons in the news lately. "He's always bitching about Alexander."

"Who's Jackson Banks?" Camilla asked.

David swiped the unlit cigarette from Dawson's mouth. "He controls the arms trade in Lake Side."

Dawson actually snarled at David, but didn't make any other aggressive moves, nor did he try to light another cigarette. Aside from himself, Victor knew David was the only other person who could do something like that to Dawson and survive.

David continued, "He has a sizable army of enforcers, and obviously the best armaments, and most importantly he brings in a lot of money for Alexander–possibly one of his biggest revenue streams. It's made Banks a little cocky. I hate to admit it, but Dawson's right. Banks is a good candidate."

Victor shook his head. "No. It's too obvious. Edward would see right through it. And though Banks is a loudmouth, everyone knows when it comes down to it, he's a coward."

"What about Marshal Samson?" David asked.

"Doesn't your city have any women crime bosses?" Camilla took a drink of her tea. "Who's he?"

Victor stared at David. He knew why his friend made that suggestion. Samson had always been someone David hated, not for any character trait or personal offense, but for the man's chosen profession.

Victor sighed. "He runs Edward's sex trafficking operation."

"He sells women and girls!" David's grip tightened on his glass, and Victor thought it might crack.

Victor shook his head. "Samson is a genuine piece of shit to be sure, and what he does is reprehensible, but the man is only interested in sex, David. He would never move against Edward. He's satisfied with his little piece of the kingdom."

"But, Victor—"

"No, David. I'm sorry."

David retreated to his brooding, and Victor knew he'd hear about this later.

"Who does that leave us?" asked Camilla.

"Aiden Walker, he runs the Lethal Games and dozens of other extralegal gaming enterprises. He works closely with Edward, and like Samson, he loves the lifestyle his role affords him. I can't see him ever turning on Edward. Frankly, he's not smart enough to pull off a coup, and Edward knows it."

"And he owes me twenty bucks," Dawson grumbled.

A tired electronic doorbell drew Victor's attention, and he glanced over his shoulder as two curious walk-ins entered the restaurant. The greeter turned them away, explaining that they needed a reservation, to their utter bewilderment.

As the door closed on them, Victor continued, "Then we have Paul Zoltan, he runs all things cyber–a real Russian hacking prodigy and Edward's prized pig. He keeps him close and somewhat isolated from the other bosses. Zoltan is the primary source of intel that Edward uses to blackmail high ranking officials. I can see Zoltan cutting and running for the right reward with the right opportunity, but I don't see him trying to take over Edward's operation."

"That just leaves Zhang Min Su," David said, breaking his silence.

"Finally, a woman!" Camilla threw up her hands.

Victor nodded. He was worried about this. From the beginning he suspected they would end up choosing Su. He knew the woman, respected her, even liked her wry sense of humor. She was in her mid-forties and had taken over her mother's operation only a handful of years ago but had taken an already successful outfit and turned it into Alexander's most lucrative venture.

"What does she do?" asked Camilla.

"Drugs," Dawson answered.

"Primarily heroin," Victor clarified. "Your father would've been working with her had he not—"

"Been blown up," Dawson finished.

Victor glanced at Camilla, unsure how she'd respond.

She stared at Dawson for a long moment before bursting into laughter. "Nothing the bastard didn't deserve," she said.

Victor relaxed. "I think it's evident, Su is our best candidate. She has a potential connection to Escarra that we can exploit, and she is hands-down the biggest revenue driver in Edward's entire organization. She's intelligent, somewhat new to her role, and she has a healthy compliment of well-trained enforcers. She's a power player for sure."

"So why would Su kill Escarra?" David drank the last bit of his water and poured another glass from the carafe the waitress left on the table. "What's our narrative?"

Victor looked down and nodded. "Su would be working to accomplish several things at once. First, she would be trying to embarrass Edward. He says he owns this city, but if someone would kill one of his important guests, for whose safety he is responsible, well, that sends a message that he isn't as strong or feared as he claims. This would create doubt in the minds of his allies and embolden his enemies."

"And that's what you told Alexander," David said.

Victor nodded.

"But there needs to be a practical purpose to this too," Camilla added. "If this Su is as smart as you say she is, the strike wouldn't just be psychological warfare."

Victor looked at Camilla, letting his eyes linger on hers, drinking in her beauty. The sense of giddy excitement she gave him was so new to him, and so exhilarating, he couldn't get enough. "You're right. What do you suggest?"

"There is a rising gang among the cartels, one led by a group of women calling themselves the *Hijas de Sangre*."

"The Daughters of Blood?" Victor translated.

Camilla nodded. "They're ambitious and aggressive. They've been attacking older, stronger cartels and toppling them. They're trying to establish themselves as a regional power. We can blame them for the bombing and claim Su is working with them. The deal could be they get all of Lake Side's drug business, and Su gets Edward's organization."

"Yes," Victor said. "This will work."

David finished another glass of water. "So how do we actually promote this narrative?"

"We follow the Daughters' tactics," Camilla said. "We use South American mercenaries to start striking and disrupting the most lucrative parts of Edward's operations—except for Su's."

"And I supply evidence to demonstrate that the explosive that killed Escarra originated from weaponry used by the cartels," Victor added.

"I'm down, as long as I get to blow shit up," Dawson said.

"And this will convince Alexander to consolidate the enforcers under you?" David asked.

"That's the goal," Victor said. "And then we'll move against Su and destroy her and her people."

David shook his head. "It's going to be a bloodbath."

Camilla frowned. "It's the price of power, David."

David shoved Dawson and made him slide out of the booth and stand, then slid out himself. In the process he accidentally knocked Camilla's glass onto the floor where it shattered. He leaned down as if to clean it up, but then stood. He stared accusingly at Victor, then turned and left.

Victor glanced at Camilla and stood to chase after David. The electric doorbell sounded as Victor pushed out of the restaurant and caught up with him on the street. "David!"

David waited for him to catch up. "Something's wrong, Victor."

"What're you talking about?"

David shook his head. "You really trust that woman?"

Victor glanced back at the restaurant. "We have a connection."

David scoffed. "Yeah, your dick."

For some reason, that made Victor angry, and he'd never really been angry with David before. He poked a finger hard into David's chest. "Don't you talk like that about my relationship with Camilla!"

David looked genuinely surprised, but the surprise faded almost immediately. "Relationship? She showed up at your apartment two nights ago, and now she's your soulmate?"

"You're the one always telling me I needed to find someone."

"Because I want you to be happy!"

"I *am* happy!" The words surprised Victor as soon as they left his lips. He'd said them before, but he'd never meant them. Not like this.

David looked at him a long moment before replying with a catch in his voice, "Victor that's all I've ever wanted for you."

"Then why are you acting like this?"

David glanced at the restaurant. "Because something's wrong. I can feel it."

"Well, until you can give me something more than a vague foreboding, you keep your mouth shut about Camilla. Is that clear?"

David stared at him for a long moment. "Yes." He turned and walked away.

Victor's churning guts betrayed his firm insistence. Something *was* wrong. He'd just pushed away a man who was like a brother to him. A man who'd saved his life when he was little, and countless times since. The only man who'd ever really cared about him.

From somewhere distant, Uncle Simon's laughter echoed, but it was only Victor's imagination–or at least that's what he told himself.

Weeks passed, and I continued to supply Jordan with names of those whose sins put innocents at risk. In each case Jordan dealt with the perpetrator in a non-lethal way, extracting confessions and leaving them... unable to continue their crimes.

JOURNAL OF FATHER KEVIN ALLEN DRAKES

CHAPTER
ELEVEN

JORDAN GLANCED down at the quivering mass that was Archibald Drexel, a high school chemistry teacher that'd been moonlighting as a drug dealer. Two of his students had been the unfortunate recipients of product laced with Fentanyl and consequently overdosed. That wouldn't happen anymore.

Jordan capped the syringe. The dose of Ketamine would be enough to incapacitate Drexel until his emailed confession brought the authorities, and hopefully it would induce visions of the grim reaper and zombie children. The broken leg and concussion would probably keep the asshole put as much as the anesthetic.

Jordan left through the back door, where he removed his skull mask in an alley but was careful not to remove his gloves until he was safe inside his jeep parked several blocks away. The high he felt with each assault was becoming shorter-lived. It was like a drug, and like a drug, subject to the law of diminishing returns. Maybe Kevin was right. Maybe this wasn't the answer. Maybe this was just a bandage for a much deeper wound.

He reached for the comfort of his challenge coin, but it wasn't there. He still hadn't found it, and it bothered him. A terrible thought had started to nag at him. What if he'd lost it at Evan Chandry's apartment? That'd been the last time he remembered having it. But if that were the case, surely some LSPD detective would've come snooping around already, because the coin was sure to have his print on it. No, he probably lost it at St. Gertrude's.

He'd spent a lot of time there recently, either receiving names from Kevin or counseling from him. He told the priest everything he remembered from his time as Thanatos's hostage, everything except for the image of him holding a bloody butcher's knife. He couldn't muster the courage to confess that piece of information because of its implications.

And there were the gaps in Jordan's memory. Kevin believed remembering what happened in those gaps would be a key factor in Jordan's healing–but he didn't want to know. He didn't want to poke that beehive. There was something ugly there, something terrible. His mind was protecting him, and Jordan didn't want to find out from what.

It was all very exhausting. Kicking the shit out of deviants was easy by comparison.

Jordan took the long way home, stopping at the liquor store and making sure to be caught on camera buying a bottle of Jameson. Once back in his Jeep, he popped the bottle open, took a swig, swirled it around in his mouth, and then spit it out on the pavement. Next he poured half the bottle out the window before recapping it and tossing it in the passenger seat. It was a ritual he'd come to perform after every mission. He'd even deliberately gotten himself pulled over once so there'd be a record of his midnight drinking. He'd been able to pass the breathalyzer because he hadn't actually drunk anything, and the patrolman had been sympathetic to a fellow vet with apparent PTSD.

Jordan finally made it home around 1:30 AM, expecting to find his apartment empty as Kate was working another all-night shift at the hospital. Instead, he found his wife waiting for him in the living room, fully dressed, their minister sitting beside her with his Bible open on his lap.

Uh oh.

They both rose as he closed the door behind him.

"What the hell is this?"

"Jordan, we need to talk." Kate was hugging herself, though her eyes were stern.

Jordan glanced at the minister. "And we need Bob here for that?"

"Jordan, I'm just here to help."

"No offense, Bob, but I don't need your help."

"Oh really, Jordan?" Kate snapped. "Then why don't you tell me where you've been?"

If you only knew.

"Kate…"

She walked up to Jordan, leaned in, and sniffed his breath. "That's what I thought."

Jordan threw up his hands. "Fine. I went out for a drink, but I'm not drunk."

"No, you're getting high!"

"What?"

Kate's eyes narrowed. "You came to see me for lunch last week at the hospital. I thought you were being sweet and trying to reconnect with me after weeks of being cold and distant. Imagine my surprise when I got asked why I took some Ketamine from the med room?"

Well, shit.

Jordan couldn't think of an excuse, so he didn't answer.

"How dare you use my access to steal drugs!"

"I'm sorry, Kate," was all he could manage. And he meant it. "But it's not what you think."

Kate threw up her hands. "What else could it possibly be?"

"Kate, why don't we give Jordan a chance to explain," Bob chimed in.

She folded her arms. "Ok, Jordan. Explain."

"Kate, I…"

You need to tell your wife. Kevin had told him on more than one occasion. *Tell her what happened to you. God gave Adam a wife to be a comfort to him, to share his sorrows and pain. This poison festers in darkness. Open your heart to her, Jordan. It's the only way to save your marriage.*

But did he want to save his marriage? The answer was yes, but the follow up question chained to it was, did he *deserve* someone like Kate? The conclusion he always came to was *no*.

Kate was Jordan's angel. She stood by him while he'd gotten sober the first time. She'd said yes when he'd proposed, knowing full well he was an alcoholic. She'd been gentle in her insistence he get help after Miguel tried to kill him. She'd been patient, understanding, and loving. She deserved to know *why* he drank. She deserved to know why he'd stolen the Ketamine. She deserved to know what Thanatos had done to him. She deserved more than anyone else to know his real name and who he really was.

Jordan had been pushing Kate away for weeks, and until this moment, he hadn't known why. But now it was clear to him. He'd been subconsciously preparing for this. Kate deserved so much better than him, and that's why he decided it was time to let her go. He was a drowning man, and he wasn't going to drag her down with him.

"Please don't report me. I'll lose my badge."

The fire faded from Kate's glare, and tears welled up in her eyes. "Is that all you care about?"

Bile rose in his throat, but he choked it back. "What I do is important, Kate."

The tears spilled out and rolled down her cheeks. "What about me? Am I not important?"

Jordan didn't answer that. Instead, he said, "You knew what I was when you married me. You knew what this life would be like."

"I married an FBI agent, not a junkie!" Kate shouted.

"You married an addict!" Jordan shouted back.

"Let's try to stay calm." Bob made soothing motions at them, but they both ignored him.

Kate shook her head and said quietly, almost to herself, "I can't live like this anymore."

"What are you saying, Kate? You want a divorce?"

"I want you to resign and get some help!"

Jordan hadn't expected that. The impulse to vomit intensified. If he was going to save Kate from himself, he had to kill any hope for him she might have. And he wouldn't know what to do without a career in law enforcement. It'd become as much a part of him as his fake identity. The truth was, Jordan Griffin didn't exist. He never really had. The man Kate married was Yuri, the acolyte of a madman. And Yuri had died when he was ten. The person who stood before her was just a shadow of Thanatos.

"No," Jordan whispered.

"No?" Kate asked, her tone incredulous. "You do get that I'm giving you an ultimatum?"

"Now wait a moment," Bob tried.

"Shut up, Bob," Jordan snapped.

"I love you, Jordan. But something is eating you up inside, and it's destroying you. I refuse to lose you to yourself."

It's too late for that.

"If you love me, I mean *really* love me, then you will leave the bureau and let me get you some *real* help."

"You mean rehab," Jordan said.

Kate nodded. "Or whatever it takes to make you well. And I promise you, I will walk every step of the way with you and stay by your side no matter how long or bumpy the road. My only ask is that you give up law enforcement, because I know since Miguel, it's only been hurting you and making everything worse. And to be completely honest, I've not been the same since that night. I can't stand the thought of losing you. I thought I knew the risks, but actually facing the crisis, well, I'm not sure I can do that again. I don't want to be a young widow, Jordan. Not from an overdose, one of your enemy's bullets, or God forbid, one of your own."

"Listen to your wife, Jordan," Bob said, and this time his words cut to Jordan's core.

All Jordan wanted to do was run to Kate, pick her up in a hug, kiss her, and promise her everything she wanted. But he couldn't. He just couldn't. Because he was broken far beyond anything she realized, and if she knew... Kevin was wrong. She wouldn't love him. She would recoil from him. He was damaged and fit only to punish the wicked. He'd been a fool to think he could lead anything like a normal life. It'd been a mistake; one Kate was paying the price for. He had to set her free.

"I'm sorry, Kate," Jordan said.

Kate collapsed into a chair, sobbing.

"If you'll let me pack some clothes, I'll go."

An hour later Jordan sat in his Jeep with a suitcase full of necessities thrown in the back. It was a little past two in the morning, and he was driving the streets, looking for a place to spend the night. At this time of night his options were severely limited. He could try to drop in on Chuck, but he didn't want to wake his old friend. He could go to Tom, but that would require a lot of explanation, and he just wanted to sleep. There were some motels that would still be checking in guests, but he didn't want to risk the bedbugs, or worse. So, Jordan settled on a parking lot. If any police hassled him, he'd just flash *his* badge, and that would be the end of it.

Jordan pulled into an empty grocery store parking lot and shut off the Jeep's engine, leaned his seat back, and tried to get comfortable, which was almost impossible. However, he was so exhausted that comfort wasn't a necessity at this point, and he quickly dropped off.

He stood next to the well outside the dilapidated mansion. It was overcast, making determining the time of day difficult. Confused, he turned in a slow circle, glancing about. How had he ended up back here after all these years? No one ever found Thanatos's hell house, and Jordan himself didn't remember where it was in spite of how hard he'd tried to find it.

Soft crying echoed up from the bottom of the well.

Jordan put his palms on its stone lip and leaned over. "Hello?" he called down.

The crying stopped.

"Who's down there?"

"Help!" echoed the voice of a small child — a little girl.

"Don't worry, sweetheart!" Jordan called down to her. "I'll get some help!"

Jordan turned to run when the little girl screamed. "No, don't go!" and broke into hysterical sobbing.

Jordan looked back down into the well. "Listen to me. I have to go get help so we can get you out of there, but I promise I'll hurry back!"

The crying stopped, replaced by an abrupt, unnatural silence.

"Sweetheart?"

The only answer was the steady drip of water.

"Hello?"

Jordan leaned further over the lip of the well and peered down into the darkness. He shouted as an invisible force shoved him from behind. He fell headfirst into the pit, striking hard against the opposite wall as he descended into the darkness. The fall was both long and fast but ended with Jordan crashing into the bottom with a splash into shallow, brackish water.

He sat up, the water only rising to his stomach. Although it should've been pitch dark, he could see what was at the bottom of the well—an old travel trunk, tipped on its side so its bottom faced him.

"Help!" Jordan repeatedly screamed at the circle of light in the distance above him.

A noise that was equal parts scratching and splashing shut him up as he froze. The lid on the trunk slid open with jerks. Jordan's heartbeat accelerated as a shuffling sound came from inside it.

A desiccated, gray hand reached up to grab the exterior edge of the trunk. The water rippled as something emerged—a small ashen form with long, stringy hair, wearing what was once a sundress, now just tattered rags.

Jordan couldn't see the dead little girl's face, but he could feel her baleful stare.

She crawled toward him, at times disappearing beneath the water, but always resurfacing, her hateful gaze never wavering. He tried to move, but his limbs might as well have been encased in ice. He couldn't breathe, he couldn't blink, he couldn't think.

The diminutive corpse climbed up his legs, then onto his chest, until her face was inches from his, separated only by a curtain of wet, stringy hair.

"I'm sorry," Jordan tried to say, but the words wouldn't form in his throat.

As if she could hear his thoughts, the girl cocked her head.

Then Jordan heard voices straight out of the past. They were the voices of a ten-year-old boy talking to a six-year-old girl.

"Do you want me to push you?" the boy asked.

She'd been sitting by herself, alone on a motionless swing.

"Yeah!" the little girl enthusiastically responded.

Tears spilled down Jordan's cheeks, and he was finally able to speak.

"I am so sorry."

A wide, gap-toothed smile appeared beneath the girl's curtain of hair. It wasn't a nice smile, but a malicious, hellish thing. Her hideous mouth began to move, and a dusty, croak-like voice said in a painfully slow cadence, "You-know-what-you-have-to-do."

Jordan woke to tapping on his window. As he'd anticipated, a police officer stood outside his Jeep. He glanced at his dash clock which reported it was just after five. Less than three hours. He yawned. It was going to have to do. He doubted he could go back to sleep if he wanted to, not with the image of the dead girl's nightmarish grin burned into his mind.

You know what you have to do.

The words were horrifyingly familiar.

Despite my protestations, Jordan continued to present himself as Thanatos. I'm not entirely sure why, but I believe it was rooted in his guilt and self-hatred, something which became clearer as he shared more of his horror story with me.

JOURNAL OF FATHER KEVIN ALLEN DRAKES

CHAPTER
TWELVE

VICTOR WATCHED on a large wall-mounted screen, the grainy green bodycam footage of a soldier moving quietly through a wood-paneled hall. The man would occasionally halt, duck down, and make hand signals to someone who was usually off camera. Now and again, they would creep up on a patrolling man in a suit and silently dispatch him, and then with equal quiet, move the body someplace it wouldn't be seen.

The footage had been pulled from the bodycam of one of the two Columbian mercenaries whose bodies now lay rolled in plastic on the floor behind Victor. Unfortunately, given Alexander's vast network, they couldn't take the chance of the men bragging about the job, thus the necessity of killing them.

David was livid when he found out they were going to double-cross them, but Victor assured him that as long as they made the payment, with a little extra to cover the loss, the mercenaries' handlers wouldn't care much if the two men didn't return. For some reason that didn't seem to satisfy David, and he stormed off before Camilla executed them.

Victor knew David hated killing the defenseless or the innocent, but in David's moral framework, these men were in no way innocent—he had seen the mercs' resume and knew what they'd done to men, women, and children. It was confusing to Victor. He, of course, didn't share David's reservations, but he did feel he understood his friend's point of view. Perhaps this was about more than just David's moral scruples. Perhaps it was about Camilla?

They hadn't spoken anymore about Victor's new relationship and instant trust in the woman, but David had been unusually withdrawn lately. And when he wasn't quiet or sullen, he was obstinate and challenged every one of Camilla's ideas or suggestions.

Victor glanced to his left where Camilla carefully studied the screen they were watching together. She'd stopped trimming her hair so that over the past few weeks it'd grown past her chin and curled at the ends.

It was beautiful.

She was beautiful.

She caught him watching her and winked. He smiled and turned back to the screen.

The grainy night-vision footage was that of a late-night incursion into Zhang Min Su's manor-house. The two Columbians were very good. They silently killed half a dozen guards and left a very frightening, very sexually charged, very unhinged letter in the bedroom of Su's sixteen-year-old daughter, along with Polaroids of the girl sleeping.

There was, of course, no danger to the girl, at least so long as they kept Dawson out of the house. He had originally volunteered to do the work they'd hired the mercenaries to do, but Victor convinced him it would be too risky, and that was true. Victor didn't voice aloud that one of the risks would be to Su's daughter.

The mercenaries had also secreted a few listening devices throughout Su's estate. Currently, Victor and Camilla were reviewing the bodycam footage more as a means of killing time until Su's daughter woke, found the threatening letter, and raised the alarm.

Of course, a crime lord like Su wouldn't call the police. Nor would she call on Alexander for help as that would be a show of weakness. What she *would* do was hire more protection and assassins to hunt down the fictional creep who was apparently stalking her daughter. Victor would make sure the threatening letters and harassing phone calls continued in order to keep Su frightened, thereby motivating her to increase her security force, which would look very much like a buildup of her own enforcer corps.

Threatening her daughter instead of her had also been a strategic decision, as Victor knew parents tended to lose their wits when the safety of their children was on the line, and he needed the usually cool and methodical Su off her game. He needed her judgement clouded. He needed her to make mistakes, mistakes like becoming reclusive to protect her daughter, which would look a lot like isolating herself from the rest of Alexander's network.

He would then feed the rumor-mill variations of a single story: Zhang Min Su was shunning Edward Alexander because she had made an alliance with the Daughters of Blood cartel, and she was building up her soldiers because she was planning on a hostile takeover of Lake Side City's Underground Empire.

It was a good plan. A realization of what he and David wanted. So why was his best friend not happy with him?

"Hey," Camilla said.

Victor glanced at her and smiled.

"You good?" Camilla shut off the playback of the bodycam footage.

Victor stifled a yawn. "It's just late." He checked his watch. "And we've got a couple hours till dawn."

Camilla grinned, stood, and climbed onto Victor's lap so she was facing him. "I know how we can pass the time."

She leaned down and started to passionately kiss him. Victor's awareness of the two corpses on the floor behind them made arousal difficult. Although a prolific killer–he'd lost count of just how many he'd slain—he had an aversion to lingering near corpses.

Thank you, Uncle Simon, for that.

Camilla apparently had no such compunctions as she became more and more animated with each kiss.

Victor stopped her. "I can't. Not right now."

The rejection in Camilla's eyes was almost enough to break his heart. She stood and sat on the corner of the desk in front of him. "What is it *mi amado*?"

Victor didn't want to tell her about Uncle Simon, not yet. But he didn't want to lie to her either. So he told part of the truth. "It's David. I think he's angry with me."

Camilla rolled her eyes. "Why do you care so much what he thinks?"

That hurt. "David's like a brother to me."

"And what has he done to earn such loyalty?"

"He saved me," Victor said.

"Like, covered your ass in a fire fight?"

Victor shook his head. "No, when I was little."

That got Camilla's attention. "Just how long have you known each other?"

Victor inhaled. "Since I was about ten, and he eleven. We met at St. Jerome's Home for Lost Children. It's defunct now, but as many of those orphanages were when it *was* in use, it wasn't a pleasant place. And it was as much the other kids who made it hell as it was the priests and nuns."

Camilla leaned forward. "Tell me what happened?"

Victor looked away from her. Why was he telling this woman his secrets? He barely knew her. Was David right? Was trusting her a mistake? He waited for Uncle Simon to say that it was, but his mind was still quiet. For Victor, that was evidence enough that Camilla was good for him, that she was a healing force in his life. That he *could* trust her.

"I was scrawny when I was ten. That attracted bullies, one of whom was an older boy named Jacob. He not only stole my food and beat on me, but he also came to my bunk at night when everyone else was sleeping and touched me."

"Oh, Victor." Camilla reached out and rubbed his shoulder.

He continued, "I told Sister Margaret what Jacob was doing, he got whipped and the molestation stopped. In my naïve ten-year-old brain I thought that meant the problem was solved, but what I'd done only made Jacob angry. A couple weeks after I'd turned him in, I was scrubbing the floor of one of the communal showers and just so happened to find myself alone with Jacob. By the time I realized the danger I was in, he was already beating me. When he took off my pants, I knew what he was going to do, but I was too small and weak to fight him off, so I resigned myself to my fate, just hoping I would survive it. And then David came. Though only eleven, David was big for his age, as big as Jacob."

"That's how David saved you?"

Victor nodded. "He'd overheard Jacob's friends laughing about how they'd changed the chore assignments so Jacob and I would be cleaning the showers together, so David ran." He chuckled. "When David was eleven, he was an awkward, chubby kid, so imagining him sprinting through the halls always makes me laugh. But he ran as fast as he could, and he got to me just in time. I'll never forget the look on his face, Camilla, when he saw Jacob hitting me and trying to bend me over." Victor shook his head. "I've rarely seen David so angry. He tackled Jacob and repeatedly smashed his head against the tile floor until blood ran into the drain." Victor met Camilla's eyes. "He killed Jacob to save me."

"How did he get away with it?"

"We told the nuns that Jacob had slipped on the wet tile and hit his head. I think they knew better, but they chose to believe it was an accident, it was easier for everyone that way."

Camilla sat sideways in Victor's lap and brushed his hair back. "I'm so sorry. I didn't realize what he meant to you."

"He's a large part of why I'm doing this, so Edward can't force him to do things that violate his conscience—so he can be free."

"And what do you get out of this?" Camilla asked. "You can't tell me you're not doing this for the power."

Why was he doing this? Why was he working to overthrow Alexander? He'd been planning it almost from the moment Alexander promoted him to chief of his enforcers. It'd been Uncle Simon's idea, though he wanted Victor to murder Alexander on the spot and to assume his identity by wearing his actual face. Truth was, Victor wasn't sure. It was just something woven into his DNA. No one could be his master, and anyone who tried had to die. It's just the way it was.

Victor didn't answer Camilla. Instead, he forced a smile and stroked her brown cheek. He moved in for a kiss when screaming from the monitor on the desk made him start. They both jumped up and leaned in close. There was no picture, just a waveform reacting to the sound; the devices they'd planted had been audio only. The screams were that of a young woman, and the frantic words that followed hysterical and in Mandarin.

"What's she saying?" Camilla asked.

Victor cocked his head. "She's calling for her mother."

After a moment of repeated screaming, another voice came over the speaker–Zhang Min Su. The two women, mother and daughter, shot frantic phrases back and forth, and Victor had a hard time translating what they were saying, but he didn't have to. The meaning was clear. They were afraid. His plan was working.

Victor smiled.

I tried every way I knew how; theologically, psychologically, logically, to reach Jordan and make him see he was as much a victim of The Mad Reaper as those he'd lured, but he continued to spiral and became even more determined to destroy himself.

JOURNAL OF FATHER KEVIN ALLEN DRAKES

CHAPTER
THIRTEEN

JORDAN WALKED into the field office wearing sunglasses to hide eyes that were red from both sleep deprivation and tears. He'd used a gas station bathroom to dress and freshen up. Tonight he'd get a motel room, maybe this afternoon if he could manage to cut out early.

Jordan made his way through the maze of cubicles, trying to avoid attention, when Morrison saw him and called him into his office. Jordan grimaced but complied. When the office door closed, Morrison took his seat behind his desk and motioned for Jordan to sit.

"You look like hell," Morrison said.

Jordan massaged his forehead. "Feel like it."

"Kate called me."

Jordan nodded. He wasn't surprised, Morrison was more than a boss, he was a family friend—they'd even considered having him perform their marriage ceremony before Kate's parents won out in their pressure to have "Minister Bob" do it. What Jordan wasn't sure of, however, was if Kate had told Morrison about his using her medical access to steal Ketamine.

"What'd she say?"

"That you'd left. And that she thinks it's the end."

Jordan relaxed. It sounded like she'd spared him, for now. Who knew what she'd do when the bitterness of time set in, and official divorce proceedings began.

"It is," Jordan said.

Morrison sighed. "Is this really what you want?"

"No!" Jordan snapped. "I love Kate!"

"Then why are you leaving her?"

"She's the one who gave the ultimatum."

Morrison removed his glasses and pinched the bridge of his nose. "Look, you know I think you're an excellent agent—one of my best. But since the incident with Agent Sandoval, you've not been yourself."

You don't know who I am!

"It wasn't just Miguel. It was Alexander getting to the brass and making them shut down our task force. It just turned everything to shit."

Morrison sighed. "Maybe it's time for you to step away. I know you're dedicated to the cause, but one day this job will be over, and then what will you have?"

Jordan narrowed his eyes. "You want me to resign?"

"I want you to really think about the long term. I want you to reassess your priorities. Is your career really worth losing your wife?"

"I can't give up. Someone has to do something. Someone has to take this on."

Morrison wrinkled his brow. "What're you talking about?"

Jordan was saying too much. He was *so* tired, and his mind was hazy. "Maybe you've been able to accept defeat, but I can't. It's just not in me. I've got to keep fighting."

"But is it worth losing a good woman who you love, who loves you? And she does, Jordan. Think of the future you're giving up."

Jordan stared out the glass wall of the office into the maze of cubicles. "I'm trying to protect her."

"From what?"

"From me," Jordan said so quietly that it could've been a whisper.

"That's it." Tom pulled open a drawer. "You need help. I'm putting you on paid leave and sending you to meet with…"

Jordan's head snapped back so fast that Morrison trailed off.

"No, you aren't." Jordan's tone was so cold and menacing that it frightened even him.

Morrison blinked, then regained his composure as his face flushed and his jaw tightened. "You're talking to your superior, Agent Griffin."

Jordan challenged Morrison's stare with his own before finally sagging and bowing his head. "Tom, in the last few months I've lost my partner, my taskforce, and now my wife. The place I need to be is here. If you take that away from me…"

"Fine." Morrison inhaled. "But you're going to meet with a doctor to get evaluated, and I'm ordering you to start meeting with a counselor twice a week. And don't think I won't suspend you if I think for one second you've become a danger to yourself or others."

"If that's what it takes to stay on active duty." Jordan stood.

Morrison stared at him, his look now devoid of anger and replaced with something different - worry?

"May I go, sir?" Jordan asked.

Morrison nodded.

As Jordan turned for the door, Morrison called out, "Jordan."

He looked back.

"You have people who care about you. Please don't push us away."

Jordan held Morrison's eyes for a beat before leaving the office. The look in Tom's eyes disturbed him. His SAC was always a self-possessed man, not prone to anxiety or worry. If Tom was showing worry for Jordan, then maybe he really was in trouble. It tracked. Jordan did feel out of control, like a truck careening down a highway, and it was only a matter of time before he crashed in a spectacular explosion. But he couldn't stop himself. He was as a man possessed, and not even his wife leaving him or the threat of losing his job was enough to convince him to step back from the edge of the abyss.

Jordan hadn't made it ten steps from Morrison's office before Agent Danielle Kelly caught up to him.

"Griffin! Where've you been? I'm drowning in cold cases, and I need your help!"

Her demanding tone irked him, and he tersely replied, "I had a personal emergency."

"Everything okay?"

Jordan shook his head. "I'm getting divorced."

Maybe that'll shut you up.

Strangely, it did. Agent Kelly was quiet a full minute before saying, "I'm sorry to hear that."

"Did you need something?"

"Yeah, actually. Can you come with me for a moment?"

Jordan wanted to put her off, but he'd already been avoiding her calls and hiding from her around the office. She'd been working cases alone that they were supposed to be partnering on. If he kept it up she was liable to register a complaint against him, and he didn't want to give Tom any more reason to pull him off active duty, so he followed her.

As they walked he reached into his pocket, once again searching for his challenge coin. He'd searched through his things again, but still couldn't find it, and now, not having access to his apartment, he could only assume he'd left it somewhere there–if he hadn't left it at Evan's apartment. He'd have to wait for when he went back to move the rest of his things out before he could really look for it. It was poetic that he'd lost it now - symbolic of everything that was going wrong in his life.

They ended up in the conference room where Kelly had laid files, documents, and pictures out across the glass table. Jordan froze at one of the images. It was Harold Jameson, the child pornographer he'd neutralized nearly a month ago.

In the image, the man's eyes were clouded over, milky white patches where his irises should be, the surrounding orbital tissue inflamed and red - burned, something Jordan had accomplished by use of industrial-strength cleaner containing sulfuric acid.

Kelly pointed at the picture. "Harold Jameson, blinded and found to be running a child pornography ring." She pointed to another crime scene photo of a bruised and bleeding man grimacing in severe pain. "Jacob Lansing, had his penis severed and then cauterized so he wouldn't bleed out, turns out he was a serial rapist." Kelly pointed to a picture of a woman with a bloody, toothless mouth. "Angie Poleman. Ran a daycare and had the living hell beat out of her. Turns out she'd been abusing her babies and even killed a couple of them."

"These aren't homicides," Jordan said flatly, though on the inside he wanted to turn and run.

"Not yet," Kelly said. "But they are clearly revenge crimes by a mission-driven perpetrator. And in several cases the victims—"

"Are they victims?"

Kelly looked at him and quirked her ruby red lips into a smile that made Jordan uneasy. "We'll call them 'targets' then."

"Targets."

Kelly went back to examining her files. "In all these cases the targets report their assailant was wearing a skull mask, and in two of them, the targets said he referred to himself as Thanatos."

"We've been over this. Thanatos was a serial killer decades ago. He's probably dead. And this person isn't killing anyone, so not our problem."

Kelly straightened and faced Jordan. "But what if our unsub was a victim of the real Thanatos? Someone who got away. Someone who knew who he was and is acting out as a way of trying to right the wrongs of the past?"

Jordan's anxiety shifted to nausea. Kelly was too damned smart.

She continued, "If I'm right, and we can catch him, he can tell us what he knows about the original Thanatos and his crimes, and then it *becomes* a homicide investigation, *the* homicide. We could finally solve The Mad Reaper case."

This is not good.

Jordan put a hand on his forehead.

"What is it?" Kelly asked.

"Headache. Look, this is all fascinating, but I can't do this today. I'm exhausted, and I need to go find a place to crash."

"I have an extra room."

The absurdity of rooming with another woman fresh off his break with Kate, and no less staying with the very woman who was apparently hunting his alter ego, made Jordan laugh out loud.

Kelly frowned. "A simple 'no thank you' would suffice."

"I'm sorry," Jordan quickly offered. "It's just that, I've been kind of a jerk to you, and you've been nothing but nice to me. I don't deserve it."

Kelly nodded. "I know you've been going through a lot."

Jordan shook his head. "You don't know anything about me."

Kelly cocked an eyebrow. "I'm a profiler."

Jordan froze. He knew that but hadn't ever put much stock into profiling. Some agents swore by it, others thought it was more akin to psychic readings and magic tricks. He'd never come down on either side.

"You profiled me?"

Kelly folded her arms and glanced to the side. "I don't usually do that with co-workers. But when you kept putting me off, I wanted to know why."

"Well, let's hear it, then."

"My profile?"

Jordan nodded.

Kelly laughed. "No, I don't think that's a good idea."

"Come on, humor me."

Kelly pursed her lips.

"Please?"

"Okay." Kelly sat on the edge of the glass conference table and drew in a deep breath. "You're focused and driven with a strong sense of right and wrong, probably religious, though you may not be dogmatic in the practice of your beliefs. You're very popular and others call you friendly, outgoing, or gregarious. Males especially gravitate toward you, whatever the circumstance: work, church, sports teams, and you're always a leader in the 'boys club.' You have a lot of friends of both genders, but few deep, intimate relationships. You're like a magician that way. You're always keeping friends distracted with your false persona, so they won't really get to know you, so they won't discover what you're hiding about yourself."

"And what am I hiding?"

"A few things, but mostly that..." Kelly hesitated, "that you're angry.

It simmers beneath the surface, always there, always ready to boil over. You've become very good at hiding it."

"And who am I angry at?"

"Yourself, mostly. In fact, I'd say it goes beyond anger and crosses into hatred."

Jordan forced a laugh. "That's crazy."

"I'm good at what I do, Agent Griffin," Kelly said with some indignation in her tone. "Others don't see it, but I do."

"So tell me, why do I hate myself?"

Kelly stared at him, head tilted. "I'm not sure."

"Best guess," Jordan said with what he hoped was a believable grin.

Kelly stood. "In reality, I'm sure it's more complex than just one thing, but if I had to guess at a root cause, I'd say you'd suffered a severe trauma. Something early on in your childhood, not so early that you can't remember it, but probably pre-adolescent, so maybe eight to ten years old."

Kelly circled behind Jordan so she was standing at his left side as she studied his face. "And mind you, this would be something catastrophic. Not a normal trauma, if there is such a thing. I mean, we're not talking about regular loss, but something anomalous, something very unusual. Whatever this trauma was, you blame yourself for part or all of it. And that guilt has become foundational to your character development, creating a compulsion in you to seek some kind of absolution or atonement. That likely shaped your decision to join the military and later the bureau, but also is the prime driver behind self-destructive and self-sabotaging behaviors like excessive alcohol use, impulsive risk taking, and probably is a factor in your divorce."

Jordan had to check to make sure his mouth hadn't fallen open. Kelly *was* good, and he had to get out of here. Any more time with this woman and she would figure out who he was and what he'd been doing.

Jordan's gaze drifted back to the files on the table, to an old news article about the original Thanatos from decades ago. He quickly looked up, but it was too late, Kelly had noticed. She stood and reached for the article. The headline read:

MAD REAPER GOES SILENT

Kelly read from the article, "Six weeks have passed without any new correspondence from the serial killer known as The Mad Reaper. This, after months of almost weekly letters containing horrific images of his victims paired with macabre poetry and nihilistic ramblings."

Kelly looked up at him, and Jordan felt naked.

"Does this mean something to you?"

"I have to go," Jordan choked out.

"Griffin?"

He rushed from the conference room, risking a glance back when he reached the elevators. Through the glass wall of the conference room, Kelly stared at him, the old newspaper held in both of her hands.

A pleasant *ding* announced the arrival of the elevator car. When the doors opened Jordan pushed through three exiting passengers in a desperate attempt to escape Kelly's stare. The jostled people didn't say anything, expressing their displeasure with scowls and angry glares, but Jordan didn't care. When the elevator doors closed, he was alone. He leaned his head against the back of the elevator and stared at the mirrored ceiling. For a split second, he thought he saw a man in a skull mask staring back at him. Then the image was gone.

His time was running out, and he thought he knew how this was going to end. Oddly, that brought a sense of relief instead of the fear it should have invoked.

In my working with and praying for Jordan it was becoming clearer that he had no intention of getting better. He did not want salvation, not physical or spiritual. He wanted to go out in a blaze of glory, and I was just enabling him. Something had to change, or he was going to do something stupid, and I would end up with his blood on my hands.

JOURNAL OF FATHER KEVIN ALLEN DRAKES

CHAPTER
FOURTEEN

VICTOR HATED PARTIES. And tonight's soiree, Alexander's latest influence peddling event, his annual Lake Side City Endowment for the Arts fundraiser, was a perfect representation of every reason why. The black-tie event took place on the top floor of Axum Tower, Alexander's high rise, and featured sculptures, paintings, photography, and art in new mediums. It was catered by a dozen of the city's finest restaurants and was attended by every important politician and socialite in the city. A bullshitters' party, David called it, and it was an apt description. For while everyone pretended to be the best of friends, they plotted how they could stab each other in the back, figuratively and sometimes literally.

Expected to be in attendance were all of Alexander's underbosses.

With the help of David and Dawson, Victor knew where each of them were at all times, it being an essential component of the security of the venue for Alexander.

Jackson Banks, the tall, dark-skinned arms dealer, was slowly circling the room like a shark, stopping at each of the bars to sample the stock. He trailed a cadre of six heavily muscled enforcers, and though guests were not permitted to have weapons, Victor was certain Banks smuggled something in.

The game runner, Aiden Walker, was dressed in a gaudy white tuxedo and planted himself dead center in the ballroom, surrounded by men and women. He waved his arms in time with whatever joke or story he was telling. Like the rhythmic waves of the ocean, laughter would erupt from his crowd, and more people slowly gravitated to his orbit. His enforcers were there too, but they were much less obvious than Banks'.

The wiry blond, Paul Zoltan, stayed close to Alexander and had only one bodyguard. He didn't do much socializing and looked as uncomfortable as Victor felt when forced into social situations.

Marshal Samson, a squat muscular man with a crew cut and a thick neck, sat in a semi-circular booth at the edge of the room with five heavily make-upped young women surrounding him, all dressed in sleek fitting, lowcut evening gowns. One sat in his lap and couldn't have been older than twelve, as indicated by the heavy rouge on her cheeks and the padding in her bra.

Another man sat at the booth with them. He had gray hair, was portly, and looked to be in his mid-fifties. Victor recognized him as Congressman Robert Hensley. The girl sitting in Samson's lap moved to sit in Congressman Hensley's lap. The politician sniffed her hair, and started getting handsy with the girl, and although she forced a smile, it was plain on her face she wanted to be anywhere but there.

David sidled up next to Victor. "That son of a bitch," he growled. "Every year the girls Samson brings get younger and younger."

"Focus, David," Victor whispered. "You're distracted and missing the most important thing."

"What's more important than that piece of shit pimping out children?" David snapped.

"Zhang Min Su isn't here."

David glanced around. "I'll be damned."

Victor smiled. "Take comfort in the fact that you're one step closer to being able to put a bullet in Samson's head."

"Has Alexander noticed?" David asked.

Victor glanced at Alexander who was near the center of the room speaking with a group that consisted of a high-ranking judge, a senator, and several wealthy businessmen.

"I'm sure he has."

"Oh, before things get um... *going*," David said, "I have an update about the Thanatos vigilante."

Victor shot David an expectant glance.

"The police found an Army Ranger's challenge coin at the scene and were able to pull a fingerprint. You're never going to believe this, Victor, but the maniac running around attacking deviants and wearing a skull mask is Agent Griffin."

Victor laughed. "Guess losing Pierce and the task force really drove him over the edge. How does he know who to target? Part of our deal with Senator Chandry was to cover for his son's more serious indiscretions."

"After the print came back as Griffin's, I put a tail on him. There's a priest at St. Gertrude's that Griffin has been seeing–Father Kevin Drakes. Evan Chandry attended that church. We believe Drakes is supplying Griffin with the names of parishioners who've confessed their crimes, and then Griffin goes after them."

"Clever." Victor was genuinely impressed. "Who else knows about this?"

David reached into his pocket and showed Victor the small bronze coin. It was engraved with a shield and lightning bolt and the phrase *Rangers Lead the Way*. "I made the rest of the evidence implicating Griffin disappear, and the detectives who know are on our payroll." David put the coin back in his pocket.

"Thank you, David."

Dawson's voice crackled as it came over the earpiece. "Any more of those tiny wieners left?"

Victor rolled his eyes. That was the code phrase Dawson insisted on using.

"It's time, David." Victor pointed at Jackson Banks. "I think Banks is armed. Please go make sure he doesn't interfere."

David glanced at Samson laughing with the congressman as the man continued to grope the twelve-year-old girl. "How do you expect me to do that?"

"I don't know, tackle him or something!" Victor pointed at Banks, who was conveniently in the opposite direction from Samson.

David moved off toward Banks. Victor wasn't really worried about Banks firing off a few shots, what he was worried about was David taking the opportunity afforded by the coming chaos to kill Samson. This way he probably wouldn't be able to do that… probably.

"I repeat, any tiny wieners?" Dawson said again, this time sounding irritated.

Victor touched his earpiece. "Yes, there is a whole platter of tiny wieners!"

"Got it," Dawson said.

Victor began to steadily make his way through the crowd toward Alexander in a way that didn't look deliberate, as if he were simply doing another sweep of the room. When he was about ten feet from Alexander, a loud *crash* resounded throughout the ballroom. Gasps, screams, and shouting followed as glass rained down from the skylight. Victor covered his head with his arm, but a couple of falling shards nicked his face. Dozens of black cords, like long striking vipers, fell from the ceiling, and soldiers in full tactical gear repelled into the room.

Victor drew his .45 and started firing while touching his earpiece and calling out orders to his security team. Materializing from the shadows, dozens of armed men dressed in tuxedos opened fire on the intruders. Unfortunately, their small arms weren't very effective against the tactical armor of the strike team.

"I need B squad in here now!" Victor shouted over the radio.

One of the intruders landed near him, but before he could raise his assault rifle, Victor moved in, grabbed the man's head from behind, and placed the barrel of his .45 against the base of his neck just below his helmet.

The gun barked, and the man convulsed before crumpling. Victor holstered his .45 and picked up the dead man's assault rifle. He raised it and squeezed off a few bursts of cover fire while he made his way to Alexander.

"Victor, what the hell is this?" Alexander demanded.

"We need to get you to the safe room," Victor replied.

Gunfire continued as Victor's security team traded bullets with the strike force, catching a number of party guests in the crossfire. Victor spared a glance in Jackson Banks' direction to find the man on the ground, David on top of him. Victor motioned at David, who jumped to his feet and ran low through the fleeing crowd of people toward Victor's position.

Victor led Alexander toward the nearest exit. Two soldiers took aim at them, and Victor shoved Alexander behind a large column. Pieces of marble exploded in a cloud of dust as automatic gunfire tore into the pillar. Victor waited for a pause in the staccato barrage before peeking out from his side of the column and returning fire. He caught one of the men in the chest, which sent him to the ground but didn't kill him, as the man's body armor would've protected his vitals.

He was about to duck back behind the column when the second soldier jerked forward, revealing David rising from a crouch. He stomped on the man's chest, and then fired two shots into his face from his handgun before leaning down and taking the man's assault rifle.

"David!" Victor shouted as he laid down cover fire.

David sprinted to Victor's position, taking the last few steps backward to spray bullets at several soldiers who'd taken notice of them.

Once behind the column, David gripped Victor's shoulder. "What's the play?"

"B Squad is thirty seconds out. Once they move into the ballroom and engage the intruders, we extract Mr. Alexander." Victor pointed at a door to a servant's exit. "We'll head through the kitchens and then double back to the penthouse and the saferoom."

David didn't respond.

"David?"

Victor caught David staring and followed his line of sight to a figure lying supine on the floor at the center of the room. She was small, staring at the shattered skylight with unblinking eyes, a pool of red spreading out from beneath her.

It was the young girl Samson had brought to the party.

"David!" Victor shook his friend.

David looked up at Victor, his eyes wild and his face a terrifying mask of rage.

"We need to get Mr. Alexander out!"

David blinked several times and nodded.

Shouting and additional gunfire signaled the arrival of "B Squad," Victor's tactical response unit. They proved a better match for the intruders, and with heavier armaments and better gear, were able to draw their fire.

Two of Victor's tuxedo-clad enforcers joined them at their position and reloaded their handguns.

"Okay, let's move!" Victor motioned to the two enforcers.

His men took point and led Alexander, David, and a few of Alexander's guests out of the ballroom and through the servant's door. They hurried through a wide hall that wound around the room and fed into a kitchen that had been abandoned by the staff. Smoke from burning food clouded the room, making visibility difficult.

As they moved into the kitchen a woman leapt from behind a cooking station and in one fluid motion slit the throat of the tuxedo-clad enforcer in the lead. Before he fell to the floor, she spun like a dancer and stabbed her knife into the chest of the second enforcer, wrenched it free, performed a standing backflip, and landed in a crouch facing Victor's entourage.

The woman slowly stood. Her form-fitting tactical suit—the color of blood—covered even her face, so only her brown eyes were visible.

"How dare you?!" Alexander stepped forward. "You have no idea the hell you've brought down on yourselves! I'm going to make sure you—"

The woman drew her gun with blinding speed and aimed it at Alexander. Victor shoved Alexander out of the way just as a loud crack echoed off the hanging pots and pans and a force like a freight train slammed into his chest, launching him backward into David. His vision faded, and he struggled to draw a breath. The last thing Victor saw was David's panicked face staring down at him, then all went dark.

Jonny was nine again, sitting in the window box reading his favorite book—James and the Giant Peach. The sky outside was golden, made so by a summer sunset that bathed the room in a gentle, orange light.

Jenny was already asleep in her bed across the room, her Raggedy Ann doll cuddled under one arm. Jonny glanced at his bed where a Raggedy Andy doll sat. He rolled his eyes. Would the twin gifts ever stop?

He dog-eared the page of his book, set it down, and climbed out of the window box. The cool wooden floor felt good against his bare feet as he padded across to his bed. He didn't bother turning down the covers, it was too hot for covers anyway, he just climbed onto the bed, hooked one arm around his Raggedy Andy doll, and closed his eyes.

When next Jonny opened them, it was dark, but not quiet. Jenny was shaking him, crying, but doing so as quietly as she could.

"What?" he hissed.

"Something's wrong!" she sobbed.

Jonny sat up, but before he could tell his sister to go back to bed, that she was just having a bad dream, a loud scream came from downstairs, followed by a thump. He jumped out of his bed, ran to the door, and opened it just a crack. The hall was dark and quiet. Jonny risked opening the door further and stepped into the hall. Jenny followed behind him, her Raggedy Ann doll clutched against her chest, her chin down as she quietly cried. They made it to the top of the stairs, and Jonny halted.

He listened hard but could hear nothing. Then, the stairs below started creaking as someone ascended from the first floor. The intruder was carrying a flashlight, or some source of light, as it cast moving shadows on the walls. One of those shadows was long and hook-shaped, like the beak of a bird.

Jonny pushed Jenny back as a figure draped in black robes came into view. He was hooded, held a long stick with a curved blade covered in dark liquid, and had a skull's face.

"Victor!" David shook him.

Victor gasped, and the world came back into view. He tried to sit up, but a sharp pain in his chest kept him lying on his back.

"Oh, thank God!" David exclaimed.

"I'm okay, David," Victor wheezed. He fumbled with his torn white shirt but managed to tear it open to reveal a sleek black vest hidden beneath. It had a large silver tear where the bullet had struck, but there was no blood.

"Ceramic." Victor rolled onto his side and, using the leg of a food cart, managed to pull himself into a sitting position. "I was told it'd better disperse the impact, but it still hurts like a bitch! Much worse than I expected."

"Expected?"

Victor winced, as much from the pain as from what he knew was coming. He nodded.

"You *planned* this?"

"Keep your voice down," Victor snapped. He glanced around. Alexander was gone, and it appeared that only he and David remained in the kitchen. The others must've moved Alexander to his safe room and chased after Camilla. "We thought it was the best way to regain Edward's trust."

"*We*? You mean you and Camilla? I thought we were in this together, Victor."

Victor rolled his eyes. "Come on, David. You know we are."

"Then why keep this from me?"

"Honestly? Because I knew you'd give me hell about it."

"You're damn right I would have!" David stood. "What if she'd aimed for your head instead of your chest?"

"You still don't trust her?"

"Hell no, I don't trust her! And I don't understand how you can. She literally showed up on your doorstep, gave you a little action, and suddenly she gets all our secrets! Did you ever stop to think that if your trust is misplaced, it could cost us our lives? And not just us, but Anne too? Hell, it already cost that little girl back there hers!" David waved in the direction of the ballroom. "Dammit, Victor, why would you do this?"

Victor couldn't answer "because she makes the voice of my dead uncle go away," so he simply said, "Because she understands me."

"And you're willing to risk it all on *that*?"

"David, Camilla is one of us."

"No! She isn't! I had our people inside LSPD look into her–she leaves her fingerprints on more than just you."

The broken glass at the restaurant.

"You had no right!" Victor snapped.

"She isn't who she says she is, Victor! Her name isn't Camilla, it's Adriana, and she's not Escarra's daughter. Her last name is Osorio. And that's from the only record they could find, which was from an arrest in Juarez for stealing a car when she was fifteen. After that she disappears. So tell me, after learning that she's been lying to us, do you still trust her?"

Victor hesitated, and in that moment of doubt, he thought he could hear a faint echo of Uncle Simon's voice.

No! I am not going to go back to that!

"Yes, David. I still trust her."

"Unbelievable! You are unbelievable!" David turned and walked away.

"David!" Victor called, but his friend kept walking. When Victor tried to rise, the pain knocked him back down and drew a fit of coughing from him.

Jordan's sanity was hanging by a thread. I was getting ready to cut him off from any more new names and plead with him to back down. Then things took a very unexpected turn. Whether for the better or for the worse, I still can't say. All I can say is that the Almighty works in very mysterious ways, and I can't deny His hand in this. No other explanation will suffice.

JOURNAL OF FATHER KEVIN ALLEN DRAKES

CHAPTER
FIFTEEN

JORDAN PULLED his Jeep around the side of St. Gertrude's cathedral and pulled into the parking lot. It'd taken him an extra ten minutes to arrive, as he'd had to take a circuitous route. He watched the street for another five minutes to be certain there were no familiar vehicles driving by or circling the block. He'd thought he noticed someone following him in a red sedan, but after waiting a few minutes Jordan decided it was the sleep deprivation inspired paranoia and not an actual tail.

He shut off the Jeep and pulled his service weapon from its holster.

Kevin long ago made him promise to leave it outside before coming into the "Lord's House," and as much as Jordan hated it, he honored his promise. He stowed it under the seat, climbed out of the Jeep, and crossed the parking lot.

He stepped into the cathedral and walked down the aisle between pews where he found Kyle sitting, arms spread out, eyes closed, and head tilted back.

Jordan sat down next to him. "Waiting on Father Drakes?"

Kyle didn't move or open his eyes. "Yeah."

"He in confession?"

"Yep," Kyle answered.

Guess he's not a talker.

Jordan drew in a deep breath and settled in to wait. Although the pews were uncomfortable, hard wood, not padded like the ones in the churches he was used to, sleep started to creep up on him. He hadn't been sleeping lately, not even in the extended-stay motel he'd rented— not that it was the most luxurious of accommodations, but it was comfortable and clean and should've made it easy to get some much-needed rest. No, Jordan was afraid to sleep. He didn't want to see *her* again, or to hear her terrifying voice.

You know what you have to do.

"I think they have some comfortable chairs in the nursing-mother's room."

Jordan started.

Kyle was staring at him with a smirk on his face. "If you're that desperate for a nap."

Jordan ran a hand over his face. "Haven't gotten much sleep lately."

Kyle reached into his oversized, camouflage coat and produced a flask. It was a dented thing, something others might call "vintage," as it looked old but functional. He popped the lid and took a pull before offering it to Jordan.

Jordan licked his lips. "I'm an alcoholic."

Kyle shrugged, took another pull, and secreted the flask back into his coat.

"Thanks all the same," Jordan said.

Kyle replied with a grunt.

To help stave off sleep, Jordan attempted to engage him in conversation. "Do you live around here?"

"I'm staying at the men's shelter." Kyle didn't look at him.

Jordan nodded. *Well, that had been a terrible question.*

They spent a few moments in awkward silence until the jangling of Kyle's dog tags caught Jordan's attention. "You were in the service?"

"Yeah. I was a Seal."

"No shit?" Jordan said. "I was a Ranger." He about reached for his challenge coin but pulled back when he remembered he'd lost it.

"Is that right? Where'd you serve?"

Jordan leaned forward, resting his arms on the back of the pew in front of him. "Did a couple of tours in Iraq, you?"

"Three tours in Afghanistan."

"Heard that was brutal," Jordan said.

Kyle scoffed. "No, it was like spring break in Cancun, except instead of wet T-shirt contests we had claymore mines and insurgents with RPGs."

"Guys like you should be kicking up their feet in an easy chair, not living on the street."

Kyle shrugged. "Thems the breaks."

"I know it's not the same, but I'm living in a motel right now."

Kyle glared at him. "Renovation or just haven't closed on the penthouse yet?"

Irked, Jordan curtly replied, "My wife kicked me out."

Kyle nodded, pulled the flask out of his coat again, and offered it to Jordan. This time Jordan took it, opened it, and drank. He handed it back, and they resumed waiting in silence for Kevin to emerge from the confessional.

Nearly an hour passed, and Jordan had to stand and pace to prevent himself from nodding off. His back was to the confessional when the sound of the wooden door swinging open caught his attention. He turned just in time to see a muscular black man dressed in slacks and a sports jacket exit the parishioner's side of the confessional. It was David Sadler, Victor Reese's right-hand man.

They made eye contact.

Everything around Jordan seemed to freeze and all sound except for his heartbeat faded. Then in one explosive instant, the world thawed.

Jordan reached for his gun, but finding the holster empty, he switched tack and charged Sadler.

"Jordan, wait!" Kevin called out.

Jordan crashed into Sadler, and the two flew backward into the wooden booth with a *crack*. Jordan swung inward with his right arm and slammed an elbow into Sadler's chest and tried to grab the back of his neck with his left hand, but Sadler was a mountain of muscle and resisted.

"Griffin, stop!" Sadler said through clenched teeth.

Jordan flashed a manic grin and head-butted him in the nose. Sadler grunted and shoved Jordan with all his force, knocking him back a half dozen feet. Jordan stumbled and fell but turned it into a backward somersault and sprung up with fists raised.

Sadler touched his bleeding nose. "Dammit, Griffin!"

Jordan lunged a second time, striking like a viper with his right fist at Sadler's orbital socket, but he blocked it with his left arm. Jordan stepped in between Sadler's feet with his left leg, turned to the side, and brought his knee up into the big man's stomach.

Sadler grunted and doubled over.

"Jordan stop!" Kevin shouted.

Jordan grabbed Sadler's right arm and twisted it up and behind the big man. Sadler cried out as he drove him to his knees and cocked back to deliver a strike to the back of the bald head.

Stars flashed across Jordan's vision, and he stumbled to the left of Sadler. He whipped around to find Kyle rushing toward him. Before he could raise his hands, Kyle leapt into an aerial spin kick, and Jordan found himself staring at a very fine red rug with gold embroidery.

"Get up!" Kevin scolded as he pulled on Jordan's arm.

Jordan let Kevin help him stand, then rubbed his jaw as he stared at Kyle. The young homeless vet locked eyes with him and shrugged.

"Kevin, what the hell's going on?"

"That's what I was trying to tell you before you decided to act like a brainless barbarian!" Kevin glanced around the sanctuary.

Two other priests had wandered into view. One of them had a mobile phone raised to his ear.

"It's okay, Hector." Kevin motioned at Jordan. "He's police."

Jordan fished out his badge and held it up, and the priest with the phone turned away.

Kevin stared Jordan in the face. He was as angry as Jordan had ever seen him, but that anger drained away when the priest looked into his eyes. He put a hand on Jordan's cheek. "When was the last time you slept?"

Jordan brushed his hand away. "Do you wanna tell me what this is all about?"

Kevin glanced at Sadler. The large man glared at Jordan while dabbing his nose with a handkerchief.

"Not here. Come to my office. Both of you."

They began to move out of the sanctuary through a side door, when Kevin halted. "Kyle, why don't you wait here. I'll be with you in a few minutes."

Jordan glanced over his shoulder to find Kyle trailing them.

"Let him come," Sadler said. "He's obviously had training. And we need all the help we can get."

"I don't want him involved in this," Kevin snapped.

"Why don't you let him hear us out and then decide for himself," Sadler said. "Like it or not, he's a part of this now. At the very least, he's a witness."

"Father Drakes," Kyle said, "It's either this, or I go drink myself stupid and pass out on a park bench."

Kevin clenched his eyes shut and muttered a prayer before finally saying, "Fine. But this feels a lot like blackmail."

Kevin resumed leading them through the hallways to a small, book-shelf lined office with a desk and chairs. It was clean, neat, and appeared to be set up for counseling parishioners. Jordan took one of the chairs opposite the desk, as did Kyle. Sadler stood in the corner closest to the door. Kevin rounded the desk and took his place in a comfortable, if not aging, leather executive chair.

"You going to tell me what this is all about?" Jordan asked.

"Before you attacked Mr. Sadler—"

"-*Mr. Sadler* is a wanted criminal!" Jordan snapped. "He's Victor Reese's lieutenant and one of Edward Alexander's hitmen. He took Casey Pierce from me!"

Sadler stepped up to Jordan's side and slammed something down on the desk in front of him—a bronze coin emblazoned with a shield and a lightning bold and the phrase "Rangers Lead the Way."

Jordan froze. His mouth dried up, and a tightness settled in the center of his chest. His whole body went cold, and the meager contents of his stomach crept up his throat. "Where did you get that," he croaked out.

"You left it in Evan Chandry's apartment."

"I don't know what you're—"

Sadler stepped away from the desk. "Don't bullshit me, Griffin. We know you've been playing vigilante. You're just lucky one of *our* people found this coin and ran the print you left on it."

You know what you have to do.

Jordan wasn't ready. There were still things he needed to do first. But he couldn't end up a pawn for Victor Reese or Edward Alexander. Maybe he could get Sadler to take him to Alexander and he could kill the crime lord. He'd never make it back. It would be his last act. Would it be enough?

"What do you want?" Jordan asked.

"That's what I've been trying to tell you," Kevin said, and he sounded exasperated. "Mr. Sadler wants to help us."

Jordan whipped his head up to look at Sadler. "Help? How?"

"I know how your little operation works. People confess their crimes to Father Drakes, he passes that information on to you, and you target perpetrators that pose a threat to the innocent." Sadler crossed his beefy arms. "Well, I've confessed my sins to the good father, and in that confession I've named a despicable man–Marshal Samson. He's a big player in Alexander's syndicate, selling women and girls for sex. I want you to help me stop him."

"Mr. Sadler and I have been over the ground rules, we don't kill our targets," Kevin said.

"Does Reese know you're here?" Jordan asked.

Sadler looked down. "No, Victor is distracted right now."

"And how's he going to react when he finds out?"

"I don't know, and it doesn't matter." Sadler met Jordan's eyes. "Samson is a monster and needs to be stopped. I may be a criminal and a murderer, but even I have my limits, Agent Griffin. Women and children should be off limits in this game we play."

"It's not a game," Jordan snapped.

"Maybe not, but it needs boundaries all the same. Samson has none."

"If you feel so bad about what you've done, why not just turn state's witness? I'm sure we can work out an immunity deal."

Sadler laughed. "On the off chance you're *not* joking, you should know I would never betray Victor. And even if I *were* so inclined, we both know I'd never see the inside of a courtroom."

Jordan hated to admit it, but Sadler was right. He'd be dead before he could testify, just like Pierce. "And what's to stop me from just arresting your ass right now?"

Sadler laughed. "You have your coin back, but our people at LSPD have your prints, photos of the coin, and instructions to release the evidence should I be arrested. So, I'm betting you're not going to want to do that."

"If you two are done measuring dicks," Kyle interrupted, "can we get into the details of the operation?"

"Kyle, no," Kevin pled. "Please don't get involved in this."

"Father Drakes, my life isn't worth shit right now. If I can do something good, maybe rescue some little girls, maybe then... I don't know."

"We could use the help," Sadler said.

"You're coming with us?" Jordan asked.

"I want to look Samson in the eyes so he knows who it was who defeated him."

Jordan nodded. "Where does Samson live?"

"In the penthouse atop the Red Line Hotel. That's also where he does all his business. No one books a room there who isn't one of Samson's customers, so we don't have to worry about innocent guests, but the girls he traffics live there too, so we need to watch out for them. He also has a healthy contingent of enforcers."

"How many?" Jordan reached out and picked up his challenge coin. He anticipated he was going to need it and all the luck it could provide.

"About a hundred."

Jordan clenched the coin in his hand. "Three against a hundred?"

"We're not going to fight them all." Sadler glanced at Kevin. "I presume your prohibition against killing doesn't apply to self-defense?"

Kevin frowned. "I prefer no killing at all, but no. I can't ask you to lay down your life for someone who is trying to take it. Just no executions."

Sadler nodded.

"That's not permission, however, and I expect you to do all in your power to avoid situations where you would have to kill in self-defense."

"I'll just shoot people in the leg," Kyle snarked.

Jordan rolled his eyes. "I trust you can get us in."

Sadler nodded. "I can get us in the front door, but we're going to have to get creative when it comes to freeing the girls and taking Samson."

"We're going to need some heavy weapons, and probably some C-4," Kyle said.

"I can get us that," Sadler replied.

"C-4?" Kevin's eyebrows shot up. "Like the explosive?"

"Don't worry, Father Drakes. I blew shit up in Afghanistan all the time."

"Fine," Jordan said. "I'll do it. But I get to haul Samson's ass in."

"You can have him once I'm done with him," Sadler growled.

"When?" Kyle asked.

"Tomorrow night," Sadler said.

"I have a motel room over on eighth, why don't we go there and plan out the details." Jordan stood. "Kyle can stay there with me tonight."

"I'll have to rent out the neighboring rooms so we're not overheard." Sadler rubbed his broken nose.

"And you're buying a couple pizzas." Kyle stood.

The three made to leave.

"Jordan, wait," Kevin called.

Sadler and Kyle glanced back but left the office.

Jordan turned back. "What is it, Kevin?"

"I'm worried about you."

Jordan chuckled. "Isn't that your job, Padre?"

"And it's a full time one."

"Hey, this is what you signed up for," Jordan waved at a crucifix hanging on the office wall, "so don't blame me!"

Kevin silently stared at him, seeming to search for the right words.

"What is it?"

The priest glanced at the crucifix, clutched the one hanging around his neck, and sighed. "I've been thinking maybe it's time to for us to stop, and that you should check yourself into an inpatient care facility—like your wife wanted."

Jordan's chest turned white hot and he ground his teeth. "Ex-wife."

"Not yet," Kevin said. "And I'm starting to wonder if she'll even get a chance to be your ex, not before you make her a widow."

"What's that supposed to mean?" Jordan balled his fists. It was irrational, but he was enraged at the priest for guessing what was on his mind.

"You look awful and smell worse. No matter how much body spray you use, it doesn't hide the fact you're not taking care of yourself. Your cheeks are sunken, which tells me you're not eating, and the bags under your eyes tell me you're not sleeping."

"What's your point?"

"You're spiraling, and I think you…" Kevin hesitated.

"I what?" Jordan demanded.

"You want to die."

Jordan stared at Kevin for a long moment before finally asking, "Would that be so bad?"

"Your premature death?" Kevin threw up his hands. "Only for those who care about you!"

"They'd get over it."

"Should we ask them? Should we call Tom? Or Chuck? How about Kate? What about your old unit? How about that homeless man you play basketball with at the YMCA? What about me?"

Shame made Jordan look away. "Don't use that tactic on me."

"It's not a tactic, Jordan. It's the truth! You need to give up this crusade of yours and think about those who're going to have to pick up the pieces you'll leave behind if you get yourself killed or, God forbid, take your own life."

"Aren't you kind of sending mixed signals, Kevin? Helping to plan this big mission with Reese's own lieutenant, and then telling me to call it quits?"

Kevin ran a hand through his brown hair. "You three *will* do a lot of good tomorrow night and save a lot of young women from a horrible fate."

"Then what's the problem?"

"My reason for helping you, Jordan, *was* to save people. I've risked everything to do it, and I don't regret that, because we *have* saved people. What you apparently don't get is that the person I've been trying hardest to save is *you*. But it's become clear to me that you don't want to be saved. You just want to punish yourself over and over, and then you want to die."

"What do you want me to do, Kevin?" Jordan shot back.

"After this mission, I want you to stop this vigilante crusade, I want you to call Kate and beg to her to take you back and get some serious help."

Jordan looked away. "I can't."

Kevin launched out of his seat and slammed his palms down on his desk. "Why?"

Startled, Jordan looked back at the priest. "Because I don't deserve it."

"Don't deserve to be healed? To be happy? To be whole?"

Jordan didn't trust himself to answer.

"What is it that you've done that is so unforgiveable that you don't deserve God's forgiveness?"

"I've told you."

"Have you?" Kevin shook his head. "No, you've held something back. What aren't you telling me?"

Jordan turned around, unable to even look at Kevin. "I don't know."

Kevin rounded his desk. "You don't remember?"

"I get flashes." Bile rose in Jordan's throat. "Images of me holding a bloody knife."

Kevin didn't reply for what felt like forever. It made Jordan tremble. Was the tolerant, forgiving man of God going to finally reject him? He'd earned that hadn't he?

When the priest did speak, gone was his frustration. His voice was again gentle, firm, and full of compassion. "Listen to me, Jordan, whatever you did, you were just a child under duress. You were abducted and held hostage by a madman, and any violent act you committed is to be laid at his feet. You are not responsible for what he made you do."

Kevin placed a hand on Jordan's shoulder. "Jordan, whatever you're starting to remember, I don't believe you killed that little girl, and I promise you that God has forgiven you for whatever part you played in her death. So if the Lord Himself can forgive you, why can't you forgive yourself?"

"I just can't."

Kevin gently turned Jordan toward him and stared him directly in the face. "Please, Jordan. Don't let The Mad Reaper claim another victim."

"I have to go." Jordan's voice cracked. He made to leave but hesitated when Kevin began to recite a blessing.

"Sancte Michael *Archangele, defende nos in proelio, contra nequitiam et insidias diaboli esto praesidium."*

Jordan turned back just in time to see Kevin make the sign of the cross. He didn't know for sure, but he guessed it was some kind of prayer for his safety. He wanted to thank the priest but didn't trust himself not to give in to emotion, so he simply nodded.

"And, Jordan," Kevin said. "If you don't care about yourself, at least look out for Kyle. Please. For me."

Jordan hesitated before finally risking an "okay." It came out hoarse and dry.

He hadn't actually planned to seek death on this mission anyway, not when there were monsters like Marshal Samson to punish.

He shot Kevin one last look and left.

I have one card left to play. I don't want to play it, and I know Jordan will hate me, and I, myself, will lose everything, but that's the reason I'm writing all of this down—making my confession. I wouldn't be doing this if I didn't think it was the only way to save Jordan Griffin's life.

JOURNAL OF FATHER KEVIN ALLEN DRAKES

CHAPTER
SIXTEEN

"IT APPEARS your suspicions were justified, Victor." Alexander stood at one of the room's exterior glass walls staring out over the nocturnal cityscape.

They sat in his conference room where, several weeks prior, the crime lord had beaten Victor and threatened his life. It was an odd juxtaposition now: Victor receiving the closest thing to an apology Alexander was willing to give while his wound was being attended to by Alexander's personal doctor—a middle-aged man who looked to be of Indian descent though spoke with an English accent.

Victor sat on the glass conference table, naked from the waist up, with an angry red bruise turning purple over the right side of his torso.

Another odd synchronicity, ribs on the other side of his body having been broken the last time he was here.

He winced as the doctor pressed a cold stethoscope against his chest over his right lung. "Does that mean the sword of Damocles no longer hangs over my head?"

Alexander glanced at him and grunted. "The members of the strike team were all South American."

Victor nodded. "It fits. The pieces of the bomb we recovered from Escarra's car were consistent with aftermarket devices sold in Columbia." Of course that wasn't true, but Alexander wasn't going to check at this point. There actually wasn't anything to check, nothing had been recovered.

Alexander cocked an eyebrow. "Aftermarket?"

"Post fall of the Soviet Union weaponry."

Alexander chuckled. "And the woman assassin in red?"

Camilla. No, not Camilla, Adriana. Why had she lied to him?

Victor gritted his teeth. Not from the pain of the doctor now wrapping his ribs, but from the hurt of betrayal. She *would* have a good explanation, he *knew* she would.

"Victor?" Alexander asked.

Victor cleared his throat. "Yes. She is likely a member of the 'Daughters of Blood.' One of Escarra's rival cartels."

"So you think they are behind this?"

Victor struggled to focus on the conversation, and worse, to recite the lies he'd practiced in his head. His emotions were unusually unruly and distracting.

"Victor?" Alexander's voice sounded distant.

Camilla had kept back her real name, but how could Victor blame her for that. She as much as admitted to him that it wasn't her true identity. And it wasn't like he'd told her *his* real name or who he was.

"Is he okay?" Alexander asked the doctor.

"So far I've only found some broken ribs. But we should probably get him in for a CT scan to make sure he didn't hit his head."

"I'm fine," Victor said. "It's just been a while since I've been shot."

Alexander actually laughed at that, to which Victor smiled.

"To answer your questions, sir: I don't think the Daughters of Blood could pull this off alone. Not being so far removed. And what's the incentive for another attack? They already got what they wanted by killing Escarra. The deal with us broke down. No, I'm worried this goes deeper. I think one of our people is working with the Daughters."

"But why?"

Victor pretended to think about the question. "Something mutually beneficial? The insider gets help usurping you, and the Daughters get the deal you were offering to Escarra."

Alexander stepped toward him. "Who would be that stupid?"

This was the tricky part. This was where Victor needed Alexander to follow the breadcrumbs he'd dropped for him and come to the conclusion himself without realizing he was being manipulated. If Victor even hinted at accusing Zhang Min Su, it would immediately ignite Alexander's suspicion.

"I don't know. Have any of your people been acting out of character?"

Alexander ran a hand through his hair. "Su wasn't here tonight. I find that highly... irregular."

Victor inwardly exulted. Alexander had taken the bait. "Would you like me to put a watch on her?"

"Do it, and I want to know of anything out of the ordinary as soon as it transpires. Understand?"

"Yes, sir." Victor would make sure there would be plenty to report.

A generous dose of Percocet muted Victor's pain and made the trip back to his penthouse bearable, at least physically. He tried to call David several times, but each time, the call went to voicemail. He parked his sedan in the underground car park and texted David. The app showed him that David had seen his text, but no reply came. Victor punched the steering wheel and exited his car with a slammed door.

In the distance, he heard echoing laughter.

He glanced around the parking garage but he was alone. That drained away his anger and replaced it with fear. He avoided looking at the side mirrors of the vehicles he passed as he ran to the elevator.

When the doors opened on his penthouse, he found Camilla waiting for him, two empty stemmed glasses in one hand, and a champagne bottle in the other. She wore nothing but a very enticing black lace bra with matching panties.

She sashayed up to him, a wicked smile on her face. "I'm glad you're back. What's say we celebrate a perfectly executed mission?"

"You don't even know how Edward reacted."

"I assume he trusts you again, and now he suspects Zhang Min Su of trying to have him killed. Am I right?"

Victor pushed past her. "Yeah."

"Victor, what's wrong?" Camilla put down the champagne and glasses and walked up to hug him from behind.

Victor sucked in a breath. "That hurts."

Camilla chuckled and squeezed harder.

"I said that hurts!" Victor pushed her away.

"What's wrong with you?" Camilla snapped.

Victor turned to face her. "You lied to me! You're not Escarra's daughter–Adriana Osorio."

"How did you—"

"David dug into your background. There isn't much, but that alone is troubling."

A dark look passed over Camilla's face but was gone so fast Victor wasn't sure he'd seen it in the first place.

"I can explain," Camilla said.

Victor sat on the couch and extended his arms. "Then explain."

"Adriana *is* my real name. Osorio is my mother's maiden name. Escarra didn't marry her. He couldn't, because she was his daughter too! So I didn't lie to you, Victor! The man is my father, and he's also my *grandfather!*" Camilla grabbed the champagne bottle and hurled it against a wall. The neck broke off and golden liquid ran down the wall to join the puddle forming on the floor.

"My mother tried to hide me from him so I wouldn't suffer the same fate, but he found her when I was barely a woman myself, and he killed her. I lived on the street after that, running for as long as I could, but eventually I ended up serving him, the same as my mother." She stood staring at him, chest heaving, her eyes alight with a wild ferocity – it was a validating sincerity he couldn't deny. Relief quashed the doubt David had sown in his mind.

Victor leaned forward and scratched at the stubble on his chin. "Jonathan."

"What?" Camilla snapped.

"That's my name."

The fire in Camilla's eyes went out, and she sat down on the couch next to Victor. He sat back and she leaned her head on his shoulder. "I like Victor better."

He chuckled. "Do you want me to call you Adriana?"

Camilla's hair brushed his cheek as she shook her head. "I chose Camilla. My father hated it."

Victor put an arm around her.

"Why does David hate me?" she asked.

"He's just protective of me."

"He's not going to come here and try to kill me, is he?"

"No." Victor soothed. "I wouldn't let him." He sighed. "Truth is, I don't know where he is. We had an argument after the mission, and now he won't answer my calls or texts. It's eating me up inside."

"What was the last thing you two talked about?" Camilla drew her legs up onto the couch and snuggled into him.

"Why?"

"Maybe that'll give you an idea of where he is."

Victor inhaled. "Well, aside from arguing about him not trusting you, and his wanting to kill Marshal Samson, the only thing we were talking about was…"

"What, Victor?"

"I don't think it'll help me find him."

"Humor me," Camilla said in her pouty voice, and for some reason that gave Victor

pause.

Why was she bugging him about this? Not wanting the argument to flare up again, he indulged her. "Remember what I told you about the assault on Senator Chandry's son?"

"Yeah, someone paralyzed him, but it turned out he was, like, a child killer."

"Right. Well, David discovered the assailant was someone we have history with, an FBI agent–Jordan Griffin–and he's working with a priest named Father Drakes out of St. Gertrude's. Apparently, the priest is Agent Griffin's C.I. They've been working together vigilante style to target deviants who prey on innocents."

Camilla was quiet for a long moment before finally saying, "Yeah, that doesn't seem very helpful."

She pressed into his side, and a sharp pain broke through the numbing effect of the Percocet, and Victor gasped.

Camilla jumped up. "Oh, babe! I'm so sorry."

Victor leaned forward, cradling his side. "It's okay."

"Let me fix you some tea. It'll help your muscles relax."

"Camilla, really, I…"

Camilla pointed at the bedroom. "Go get undressed and lay down right now! I'll be in in a minute with some tea, and we'll take it easy so you can rest."

Victor smiled, stood, exchanged a quick kiss with Camilla, and retreated to the bedroom. He gingerly stripped down to his briefs and climbed into bed. A moment later Camilla arrived with the promised tea. She made him drink it down, then snuggled into him so he was spooning her. He must've been a lot more tired than he realized, because it wasn't long before he fell into a hard, dreamless sleep.

As if no time had passed, Victor woke to the light of dawn filtering in through the windows. Camilla was missing from the bed, but running water from the bathroom told him where she was. He reached for his phone, but movement hurt, so he glanced at a wall clock instead and was surprised to see he'd slept uninterrupted for a solid nine hours. No nightmares, no waking in a cold sweat, no disembodied voices taunting him, nothing of his usual nocturnal experiences. It was probably the best sleep he'd ever had, or at least in his living memory.

The sounds of the shower abruptly stopped. A moment later Camilla walked out of the bathroom wrapped in a towel. "You best be feeling better this morning."

"Why?"

Camilla answered by dropping the towel.

She came up behind me and put a gun to my back and then ordered me to take her to Father Drakes. He was in his office, so I took her there. She wanted information about someone named Sadler. I'm sorry I really don't remember the details, I was too frightened. She threatened to shoot me if he didn't tell her what she wanted to know. She had Kevin figured out, he wouldn't give in to anyone like that for his own safety, but if anyone else's life was on the line... Anyway, after she got what she wanted, she shot Father Drakes, then struck me in the back of the head. When I regained consciousness I called 9-1-1.

STATEMENT OF FATHER HECTOR ALVAREZ

CHAPTER
SEVENTEEN

THE RED LINE hotel was surprisingly clean and lush, not the seedy, dirty, smoke-filled den of iniquity Jordan had pictured. The lobby itself was huge, with a vaulted ceiling supported by mammoth marble pillars, its walls adorned with art, and its whole aesthetic comprised of a chic, modern décor.

The upscale, classy feel of the hotel made the whole thing so much worse. The clientele weren't unkempt, wild-eyed, drooling lechers as Jordan pictured, but well-dressed men of means. Likely executives, lawyers, politicians, government officials; and just as likely they were married with children of their own. How many of them had daughters the same age as the girls they'd come here to rape?

Jordan tightened his grip on the handle of his suitcase. It was large, with wheels, but instead of clothes and whatever depraved items a predator would bring to an illicit liaison with an underage courtesan, it contained a fully automatic assault rifle, several handguns, ammunition, concussion grenades, body armor, and, of course, his Thanatos mask. Kyle towed a similar suitcase behind him, filled with similar items, though his also included a dozen blocks of C-4 and Molotov cocktails.

That was all for later. Right now they needed to get in, and that required them to look like clients, which meant they dressed the part– Jordan in one of his nicer suits and Kyle outfitted in black slacks, expensive Italian loafers, and a cream-colored silk shirt with the sleeves rolled up, all courtesy of David Sadler's credit card. Kyle had shaved and slicked back his hair and looked every bit the part of a rich, underworld entrepreneur looking for easy sex.

They followed Sadler past the reception desk, triggering a thin, middle-aged concierge to rush out from behind the desk and intercept them. "Can I help you gentlemen?"

Sadler stopped and stared down at the shorter man. "We're heading up to twenty-nine."

Twenty-nine, "the party floor," Sadler had called it. An open floor plan that was more like a nightclub than the floor of a hotel. The setting for nightly drug and alcohol fueled orgies, and the place they were most likely to find Marshal Samson.

"I'm sorry, I'm afraid that's off-limits. And for that matter, this is a reservation-only hotel. We don't accept visitors or walk-ins."

Jordan admired the man's courage, standing up to the much bigger and much more intimidating Sadler–though he figured that was because the concierge had an armed security team at his beck and call.

Sadler smiled, and it wasn't at all friendly. "Do you know who I am?"

The concierge faltered. "I'm afraid not."

Jordan glanced at the reception desk where another concierge was staring with her mouth hanging open. She shook herself from her stupor, touched her earpiece, and whispered something. The concierge turned his head to listen, and his eyes widened. He looked up at Sadler as though seeing him for the first time.

"I am so sorry, Mr. Sadler. Are you here alone tonight, or will Mr. Alexander be joining us?"

Sadler glanced at Jordan and Kyle. "I'm escorting these two VIPs for Mr. Alexander. They're heading up to twenty-nine."

"Of course! Let me tell Mr. Samson you're coming." The concierge reached for his earpiece.

Sadler placed a firm hand on the man's wrist. "These two are personal friends of Marshal's. It's supposed to be something of a surprise."

He nodded vigorously. "Yes, of course. I'll take you up myself." He waved at Jordan and Kyle's suitcases. "Would you like me to have someone bring those up for you?"

"No!" Jordan blurted out to the surprise of both Sadler and Kyle. He glanced at Sadler and then looked back at the concierge and forced a smile. "We've got them."

"Very well," the concierge acquiesced. "If you'll follow me?"

He led them through the lobby to a hallway filled with chrome elevator doors. A pair of beefy security guards lurked in the corridor, dressed in expensive black suits. They eyed Jordan as they stood waiting for the next elevator car. Once the car arrived, the concierge waved a blue keycard in front of an R.F. pad to the right of the elevator doors, and the doors opened with a pleasant *ding*, revealing an overweight man well into his fifties straightening his tie while looking at his reflection in the elevator car's mirrored interior. Jordan quickly looked away.

It was Assistant Special Agent in Charge Adam Seigers.

"Griffin?"

Shit!

Jordan looked up and met the man's eyes.

"Son of a bitch!" Seigers said. "Well now I know why you can't stay awake in my morning briefings."

Sadler reached for his gun, but Jordan touched the big man's arm, and he stopped.

"Seigers," Jordan replied. "I can't say that I expected to see you here."

Seigers laughed. "Man's gotta blow of a little steam now and again, and I can get things here that my old lady just won't give me."

That made Jordan sick. "You're not going to tell Tom about this are you?"

Seigers laughed again. "You keep my secret, and I'll keep yours."

Jordan forced a smile. "Hey, Adam, can I call you Adam?"

Seigers nodded. "You can here, but if you try it in the office I'll bust your ass!"

Jordan fake laughed. "We're heading up to twenty-nine. Why don't you join us?"

Seigers raised his eyebrows. "You *do* have friends in high places, don't you? Hell yeah, I'd love to! I was just heading down to the bar for a break between sessions. Thanks to the 'little blue pill' I'm good for two or three girls these days."

"Well, come on!" Jordan stepped into the elevator with his suitcase in tow.

The other three men boarded behind them, and the concierge touched his key card to another R.F. pad and pressed the button for the twenty-ninth floor.

"So, what did you order, Griffin?" Seigers asked with a knowing grin. "What's your guilty pleasure?"

Anger ignited in Jordan's chest, and bile rose in his throat. This man, someone who'd sworn to enforce the law, was talking about captive human beings, in many cases children, as though they were items on a restaurant menu.

"I'm not sure."

"Come on, spill it!" Seigers slapped him on the back. "We're both foxes caught in the hen house. I won't kink-shame you."

"I'm still new to this," Jordan said.

Seigers leaned in so he was talking low into Jordan's left ear. "Then let me give you some recommendations. You ought to ask for China Doll. Gorgeous and *young*! And she does a really hot daddy/daughter role play."

Jordan let go of his suitcase, whirled, and slammed Seigers into the back wall of the elevator car so hard the mirror cracked. Seigers' eyes widened and he opened his mouth, but Jordan didn't give him a chance to speak. He pummeled Seigers, striking over and over until the man's face was a bloody pulp.

"Griffin!" Sadler barked.

Jordan stopped and Seigers slumped to the ground, unconscious.

Well, now there really wasn't any going back. That was for damned sure.

Jordan turned to find the concierge wide-eyed, mouth hanging open. Kyle hit the emergency stop on the elevator control panel, halting the car on the twenty-second floor.

"What are you doing?" the concierge asked.

Sadler stepped behind the man and snapped his neck with swift, brutal efficiency, letting his corpse crumple to the elevator floor.

Jordan drew his .45 and trained it on Sadler's head. "What the hell, Sadler?"

"A little much with the innocent concierge, don't you think?" Kyle added.

"Innocent?" Sadler laughed, but it was devoid of mirth. "No one here is innocent. How do you think Samson ensures those who work here don't report what they know to the cops or the press? Threats only go so far, especially when someone sees the horrors that go on in this place. No, everyone here is a participant."

Jordan lowered his gun.

"His name was Dennis Evans," Sadler said. "There's a smaller, more niche establishment that Samson runs called The Nursery, and it's not a floral shop. Evans was a frequent patron there before hiring on here."

Jordan re-holstered his gun and stared at the corpse. "A pedophile."

Sadler nodded. "And everyone here is tacitly encouraged to test out the merchandise. That way they have an interest in keeping Samson's secrets, because it's also their secret."

Jordan had promised Kevin they wouldn't kill except in self-defense. This was a clear violation of that promise, but he didn't feel guilty. The dead man on the floor of the elevator deserved what Sadler had done to him.

Kyle checked his watch. "We have to move."

Jordan removed his suit coat before picking up his suitcase and roughly dropping it on Seigers' chest. The unconscious man groaned, but Jordan didn't care, he needed the space and the traitorous piece of shit deserved it. He unzipped the suitcase and donned the camouflaged flak jacket, radio, and earpiece. He loaded the pockets with spare magazines of ammunition, smaller guns, and some flashbangs. He glanced to his side to find Kyle doing the same, except the former Navy Seal had a large duffle bag full of C-4 and bottles of gasoline stuffed with shredded motel towels.

The plan was for Kyle to ascend to the hotel's roof and use the explosives to take out the building's water towers in order to cripple the fire suppression system, that way when they set the fire the sprinklers wouldn't extinguish it. Pulling the fire alarm was Jordan's idea, to clear the building and give the enslaved girls an opportunity to escape, while getting the attention of the fire department. But to prevent someone from canceling the alarm, and to invite the attention of the press, the fire had to be real. It was risky, and people were going to get hurt, and they themselves may not make it out, but it was worth it if they could bring down the hotel and liberate its captives.

"Ready?" Sadler asked.

Jordan grabbed his skull mask and fitted it over his head and onto his face before nodding.

Sadler rolled his eyes. "You might as well wear a name tag."

"What're you talking about?"

"If anyone digs into your past, they're going to figure it out." Sadler swiped the keycard, pressed the button for the twenty-eighth floor, and the elevator lurched back into motion.

"You don't know what you're talking about!" Jordan snapped.

Sadler chuckled. "I know more than you think."

What did *that* mean?

Before Jordan could ask, the elevator doors opened onto a long hall lined on both sides with hotel room doors.

"This is my floor." Kyle pushed past them and stepped out of the elevator.

He produced a flask and took a long pull before making it disappear beneath his flak jacket with the flourish of a magician.

"Are you drunk?" Jordan shared a concerned glanced with Sadler.

"And a little baked."

Sadler handed the keycard to Kyle and motioned toward the stairs to the right of the elevators. "Roof access is two flights up."

"See you on the other side." Kyle threw a sloppy salute and dashed off through the door and into the stairwell.

Jordan said a quick mental prayer for Kyle's safety, not based on *his* faith, but on the faith and request of Kevin, who'd tasked him with watching over Kyle. Thinking of the priest caused ice to blossom in his chest. It was different than the manic adrenaline the mission produced–something he was used to from his days in the service and time in law enforcement. No, this was a feeling that something was wrong. He couldn't shake it, and that disturbed him.

"Ready?" Sadler asked.

Jordan pulled two flashbangs from his flak jacket and thumbed off the pins. "Yeah."

Sadler pressed the button for the twenty-ninth floor.

The elevator lurched, and the glowing numbers on the display turned over from twenty-eight to twenty-nine, and the car stopped with a chime. The chrome doors parted like a curtain, revealing a wave of pulsing bass and a huge open space, like a dance floor. It was dark and thick with smoke from both the effects machine and whatever people were smoking. The only light came from the multi-colored flashing strobes mounted to the ceiling. It was like a rave, except at this party, instead of strung-out dancers flailing themselves across the dance floor, there were dozens of couples and groups of people in various states of undress, clumped together on couches, in booths, and even on the floor, engaged in just about every form of sex one could imagine.

Jordan ground his teeth.

This was evil.

Righteous rage welled up inside of him, and he tossed the flash-bangs into the room. He and Sadler ducked back into the elevator and covered their ears. A beat passed before a flash of light washed over them, followed by two explosions that thrummed through him. Jordan uncovered his ears to screams and shouting.

Sadler's lips formed the word "Go!" and he pointed into the room.

Jordan reached for the assault rifle slung over his shoulder, bent low, and began to move into the room like the soldier he used to be. It was amazing to him how easily it all came back to him.

Sadler neither wore a flak jacket nor carried an assault rifle. Instead, he drew two silverplated .45s and moved into the room, breaking right, opposite Jordan.

They passed crying women and naked men rubbing at their eyes. Jordan went out of his way to slam the butt of his rifle into the jaw of one man who pawed at him from the floor. The resultant *crack* was very gratifying.

Shots rang out above the music. Jordan scanned the area. Five men in suits emerged from the smoky shadows at the far end of the room. Sadler pivoted, took aim with his right handgun, and fired. The man who'd opened fire fell, and his four remaining companions exploded into sprints straight toward Jordan and Sadler.

Jordan took aim with his assault rifle and nearly pulled the trigger, but he couldn't bring himself to do it. He'd promised Kevin. And despite everything, despite his readiness to throw it all away, he couldn't break that promise. So instead, Jordan aimed his assault rifle just above the charging bodyguards, switched the gun to full auto, and squeezed off a burst of automatic fire as he broke into a charge of his own.

The four men in suits halted their charge and ducked down, looking for cover. Jordan continued his sprint toward them, crossing the distance so quickly they didn't have time to scatter. He leapt into them, swinging his rifle butt first into the face of the closest bodyguard. The man cried out, his deformed jaw hanging at an awkward angle. He wouldn't be getting back up.

Jordan didn't stop. He pressed forward, channeling all his rage into each strike as he laid into more of Samson's bodyguards. Using his assault rifle as a club, he struck a second man in the stomach. The man doubled over, and Jordan brought the butt of his rifle up into the man's chin so hard he knocked out two teeth in a spray of blood. Jordan whirled and sank the barrel of his rifle an inch into another bodyguard's shoulder and pulled the trigger. Jordan's rifle shook and the man screamed as a chunk of blood and bone exploded onto the man behind him.

Covered in the blood spatter of his colleague, that man managed to recover and level his .357 Magnum at Jordan's head.

Jordan froze.

A *crack* from behind made him start, but instead of a bullet blowing Jordan's head off, the bodyguard aiming his pistol at Jordan fell to the ground, part of *his* head missing. Jordan glanced behind him to find Sadler lowering one of his silver-plated guns.

Jordan nodded his thanks, and the two rushed forward.

By this time, all of floor twenty-nine's patrons, both clothed and unclothed, had retreated to the elevator and were desperately slamming the call button. There were stairs, but the low light apparently made those hard to see, and most of the crowd didn't find them.

Sadler led them to a large booth at the far side of the room next to an elevated DJ's table. Sitting at the booth, drinking a beer, was the short, thick-necked form of Marshal Samson.

Jordan didn't like the man's calm demeanor and honestly, the bass-heavy music was giving him a headache, so he aimed his assault rifle at the DJ table and unloaded a full magazine on the equipment until the music stopped. That did make Samson start, but he still didn't move from his spot.

"David Sadler," Samson finally said. "Does Reese know you're here?"

Sadler grinned. "Get up, you son of a bitch."

Samson took another drink of his beer, then started to stand.

"Hands!" Jordan shouted.

Samson glanced at Jordan.

"Let's see your hands."

Samson smirked and raised his hands, showing that they were empty.

"Step out of the booth." Sadler motioned with the gun in his right hand.

Samson laughed but complied.

"You surprised me, David," Samson said. "I didn't think you'd be so ballsy as to come in through my front door."

Samson's words stunned Jordan. He knew they were coming? Samson knew they were coming…

"Sadler!" Jordan called, but it was too late.

Automatic fire rang out from behind them. Sadler grunted, lurched forward, and stumbled to the ground. A dozen soldiers armed with automatic rifles and decked in tactical gear emerged from the smoke at the front of the room near the elevators.

Oh shit!

Jordan tossed another flashbang at the oncoming soldiers, turned his back to the explosion and used the moment of confusion to eject the empty clip from his assault rifle and slam in a new one. The blast of light accompanied by the concussive wave caused the advancing force to halt and scramble for cover which bought them some precious few seconds.

It had been a trap. Samson knew they were coming. But how?

On his periphery, Jordan caught Samson draw a handgun from his rear waistband, step over Sadler's prone form, and aim it at that back of his head.

You know what you have to do.

Yuri sat in his kennel, scraped knees drawn up to his chest, shoulders covered in a thread-bare, dirty blanket. He rocked back and forth and sobbed. Not only had he lured the little girl to this awful place, but Thanatos—that's what the tall, skinny, pale-faced man made him call him—made him bring her into the house and up to his Science Room. He'd made Yuri watch as they did awful things to her, things that made her bleed and scream. Finally, when she stopped screaming because she had no more breath in her and her eyes stared at nothing, Thanatos made Yuri put her in the trunk and take her to the well.

Yuri still had blood all over him. When he asked if he could take a bath, Thanatos dumped a bucket full of the little girl's pee on him. So now Yuri stank of pee and blood. He bowed his head and sobbed harder.

At first it'd just been grown-up women, like his mom, then some teenagers like his sister, and even a few boys, but Thanatos kept talking about how he wanted a little girl, and how Yuri was going to help him catch a little girl.

Yuri had told the monster "No," but that ended with him on Thanatos's

"Science Table." And after just a few minutes of "Science" Yuri gave in and promised he would do what Thanatos said–he would help him get a little girl.

Now Yuri hated himself. He should've just died. But he was too scared, and Thanatos's "Science" hurt so bad.

The only comfort in the nightmare was a black-haired boy about his own age who was also the captive of Thanatos. When Yuri wasn't forced to be in his kennel, he and the boy were actually allowed to play together, and sometimes it was almost like they weren't the slaves of a madman.

But there was something odd about the black-haired boy. For some reason he didn't have to sleep in a kennel. He also had a twin sister who Yuri rarely saw. She mostly stayed in her room, and the few times Yuri did see her, she didn't talk. Thanatos treated her very differently, almost as if he didn't care about her, but the black-haired boy did care about her. He was very protective of his sister. Yuri guessed that maybe the reason the boy helped Thanatos hurt others was so the monster didn't hurt his sister. But for some reason it didn't make the boy cry like it did Yuri.

The hinges of the basement door whined and the door creaked, announcing the coming of a visitor. Yuri looked up to find his friend, flashlight in hand, carefully making his way into the basement.

The boy knelt in front of Yuri's kennel. "You okay?"

Yuri shook his head.

"I'm sorry, Ree." The boy produced a ring of keys from his pocket. "He wants you to get cleaned up."

"Why?" Yuri asked, though he thought he knew the answer already.

"We're going out." The boy unlocked the padlock on Yuri's kennel.

"For another girl?"

The boy grimly nodded.

"No. I won't do it." Yuri vigorously shook his head.

"He'll kill you, Ree!"

Yuri didn't say anything.

"Please," the boy begged.

Yuri climbed out of the kennel on his hands and knees, stood, and followed his friend up the basement stairs. He was allowed to shower and change into fresh clothes, then eat cold, two-day-old chicken. It had a few cockroaches already feeding on it, but Yuri was so hungry he didn't care. He had just barely finished eating when Thanatos came into the dirty kitchen.

"School's almost out. We best be going."

Yuri thought of the blonde little girl on Thanatos's "Science" table, and he could swear he still heard her screams. It made him want to cover his ears. The sound woke something in his little-boy heart, a fire that burned away his fear and grief.

Yuri stood and shook his head. "No. I won't help you anymore."

"Yuri!" The black-haired boy tried to grab his hand and pull him forward, but Yuri shoved him away.

Thanatos turned around, his blue eyes boring down into Yuri. "You won't?"

"No!"

Thanatos stared for a long moment, and Yuri's nerve started to crumble. But he thought of the little girl with her hand in his, walking up the grand staircase toward the "Science Room," and the flames inside him burned higher.

Thanatos finally smiled. "How very brave. But I am not going to stop my experiments. And if you won't help me, I will have to kill you like I did your little girlfriend."

The tall, sallow man rounded the table and reached into a kitchen drawer from which he produced a large butcher knife.

Yuri's heart pounded faster.

"Let's see just how brave you really are."

"Yuri," the black-haired boy whined from behind him.

Thanatos placed the knife on the table next to Yuri. "If you want to live and you want to stop me, you know what you have to do." He stretched his arms out, presenting his chest to Yuri. "The question is, are you brave enough to do it?"

Yuri looked at the knife, and his fingers twitched. He'd never killed anything larger than a rat, and even that had bothered him. He glanced at the knife and then up at Thanatos.

"You know what you have to do," Thanatos repeated.

Yuri tried to reach for the knife, but the fire inside him had dwindled, and he just couldn't do it.

Thanatos sneered at him and brought his fist down, striking Yuri in the face. Yuri fell against the table so his upper body lay on it. Blood dribbled from his nose.

"That's what I thought." Thanatos laughed. "Now go get in the car!"

Tears mingled with the blood pooling under his cheek, and Yuri imagined the *little girl in the trunk at the bottom of the well. Would she have company soon? How many more little girls could fit down there? His vision cleared and the first thing he saw was the butcher knife in front of him.*

You know what you have to do.

Yuri reached for the knife, stood, gripped the handle with both hands, raised it above his head, and flung himself at Thanatos. The tall man didn't even have time to turn around before Yuri plunged the knife between his shoulder blades. Thanatos arched his back and sucked in a breath, then stumbled forward and collapsed.

Yuri leapt on top of him, and with strength that belied that of a ten-year-old, he wrenched the knife free and stabbed over and over and over again. He would make certain this monster would NOT get back up, would NOT hurt any more girls. He sobbed and screamed and stabbed until he finally heard his friend calling his name.

"Yuri! Yuri! Stop!"

Yuri turned to find his friend shouting at him.

"Ree, he's dead," the boy said.

Yuri looked down at Thanatos. There was so much blood. Too much blood for the man to remain alive. His friend with the black hair was right. Thanatos was dead. Yuri had killed him.

Jordan had killed Thanatos. He had done it to protect the lives of others. He had killed to save lives. He hadn't killed any children. Those flashbacks of him holding the bloody knife were fragmented memories of when he had killed The Mad Reaper.

You know what you have to do.

It wasn't about suicide. It was about doing what needed to be done to save lives. Something inside Jordan, the broken piece, the thing that made him want to die, slipped back into place, and the self-destructive madness retreated. It was like in the Bible when leprous men were miraculously healed or the sight of the blind was restored. He wasn't entirely whole, but Jordan felt as though he'd stepped back from the edge of the abyss.

Solid in a way he hadn't been for weeks, Jordan turned, aimed his rifle at Samson's thick head, and fired.

The squat, muscular man pitched sideways and crumpled to the floor next to Sadler.

Jordan flung another flashbang—his last–in the direction of the approaching soldiers and ran over to Sadler, who'd rolled over and was coughing and struggling to sit up. He quickly checked the big man but found no blood.

"Ceramic," Sadler answered Jordan's quizzical look. He touched something beneath his shirt.

Jordan's earpiece crackled, and a tinny version of Kyle's voice said, "Hey, guys, I've got a problem."

Automatic fire ricocheted off the floor and walls near Jordan. He touched his earpiece and replied, "You're not the only one."

Kyle ignored him. "There's a bitch dressed all in red up here on the roof trying to stop me from blowing the water towers! If ya'll are done dispensing justice, I could use some help. Ouch, dammit that hurt!"

"Camilla," Sadler spat.

"You know who that is?"

Sadler nodded. "Now we know who tipped off Samson."

"What does she want?"

"I'm guessing she wants me dead." Sadler found one of his silver-plated .45s and climbed into a crouch. He fired three shots at the approaching soldiers who'd carefully fanned out in an effort to flank them.

Jordan fired off several shots in the general area of the soldiers. He'd killed the overpowering music, but the strobing, multi-colored lasers and the smoke machine still made it difficult to see.

"We need to get to the roof," Jordan said.

"We need to get out of here." Sadler rose and fired off three more shots.

Jordan tore off his skull mask and glanced around the room looking for an exit. The closest green glow of an exit sign was on the other side of their assailants.

They were trapped.

Two bullets struck behind them and one caused a spiderweb of cracks to form on a tall floor-to-ceiling window. Jordan looked out the window next to it. They were nauseatingly high up from the street, but there was a ledge that ran along outside the building that terminated against a corner block–a very climbable cement block.

"How far up is the roof?" Jordan shouted over the sound of escalating gunfire.

"Two flights," Sadler replied. "But I told you..."

Sadler didn't have time to complete his thought as Jordan turned his fire on the already damaged window and finished blowing the glass out into the open night air with a barrage of automatic gunfire.

"Come on!" Jordan shouted.

He climbed out onto the ledge; its width was not much more than eighteen inches. Above him he could see the roof and a very scalable terrain of architecture. He slid along the building toward the corner block.

Sadler stuck his head out of the broken window and shouted at him, "Are you insane?!" The big man fired twice more behind him, and that was enough to convince him to step out onto the ledge.

"Just follow me and do exactly what I do," Jordan called back.

A stream of curses, mostly starting with the letter "F", flowed from Sadler's lips as the two made their way up and over the first block. A couple brave soldiers stepped out onto the ledge and fired at them, but aiming while trying to keep your balance on an eighteen-inch ledge was apparently difficult, and none of the bullets even came close, and they quickly abandoned their attempt.

When they made it to the thirtieth floor, Jordan tried to shoot the windows so they could get in and access the roof via stairs or elevator, but those windows turned out to be made of bullet-proof glass. It made sense, as that was the penthouse and Samson's personal living space. So they continued to climb.

Jordan had some experience in the service with free-climbing, and he also used to do it for fun, and he was impressed with how well Sadler kept up. The big man's swearing and attitude made it obvious he hadn't done much climbing, if any, but he was handling the stress of it exceptionally well—he only slipped twice and never bad enough to lose his grip entirely. Chalk it up to adrenaline and self-preservation, or if Kevin were here, he'd say divine intervention.

Kevin.

Jordan still had that nagging cold feeling in his chest. He would need to check on his priest-friend as soon as he could.

Jordan crested the roof and pulled himself up over the lip just in time to see Kyle take a roundhouse kick to the face from a hooded woman dressed in form-fitting tactical suit. The former Navy Seal impressively spun with the force of the kick, spinning intentionally so he didn't fall. Kyle appeared loose and flexible. He held a device in his hand with a short silver antenna and a homemade switch. The remote detonator.

Jordan glanced at the mammoth water towers perched on stilt-like footings, bricks of C-4 fastened into place beneath each of them. Kyle had finished rigging the tanks to blow, and the woman, Camilla, Sadler had named her, was trying to take the detonator from him.

Jordan reached down to help Sadler up onto the roof. Sadler brushed off his slacks, drew his one remaining silver plated .45, and aimed it at the woman.

"Camilla!" he shouted.

The woman stopped her martial advance on Kyle, looked down at them, then kicked Kyle in the chest. He fell off the upper level upon which they'd been fighting, to a lower level and out of sight; the remote detonator flying out of his grip and sailing in another direction. Jordan followed its trajectory, and though he didn't see where it landed, he thought he knew the general area.

Look out for Kyle. Please, for me. Kevin's words came back to him.

Jordan searched what he could see of the roof for the younger man but didn't see him.

Camilla turned and took a few steps toward them. She removed her hood and mask, revealing a young, pretty Latina woman with brown, shoulder-length hair.

"David." Camilla smirked.

"Does Victor know you're here?"

"He's sleeping, soundly. And when he wakes up, he'll find me next to him as he always does."

This was Reese's lover? Jordan slowly reached into his flak jacket and retrieved a full magazine and tried to surreptitiously unsling his assault rifle.

As if Camilla could read his mind, she looked straight at him. "Is this your vigilante FBI agent?"

"What are you doing here?" Jordan shouted. "Didn't trust Samson to get the job done himself?"

Camilla frowned. "I'm not about to let you wreck such a lucrative revenue stream."

"Why do you care?" Sadler retorted.

Camilla raised her eyebrows. "Why do I want to protect my interests?"

"*Your* interests?"

She smirked, and it would've been attractive if her smile hadn't been full of malice. "Well, it *is* going to be *my* empire."

"You conniving bitch! You've been playing us all along!" Sadler shouted.

Camilla grinned. "Not you, David. You never trusted me."

"Do you even care about Victor?"

She shook her head. "But it's not his fault. I'm just not into men."

Automatic gunfire rang out, and bullets ricocheted off the stone lip behind Jordan.

"Shit!" he shouted, diving for cover. Camilla had been stalling, waiting for the rest of Samson's men to make it to the roof.

Sadler didn't take cover. He fired on Camilla, but she was too fast and something of an acrobat. She did a standing backflip, landed in a crouch, and in the process somehow produced two handguns. She returned fire, and Sadler took a bullet in the shoulder, spinning him to the left and knocking him on his back.

Jordan unslung his rifle, swapped out the magazine, stood, and blasted short bursts of gunfire as he crossed over to Sadler.

"No ceramic this time?" Jordan asked.

Sadler shook his head. "Took me in the left shoulder."

"Can you still fight?" Jordan took aim at a man in tactical gear who'd climbed up where Camilla had been. She'd vanished in the few seconds Jordan had taken to run to Sadler. Jordan fired, taking the soldier in the face, and he went down.

Sadler groaned as he struggled to stand. Jordan helped him to his feet then found his gun and put it back in the big man's hand. More of Samson's soldiers fired on their position, forcing them to take cover behind a large, boxy metal casing.

More gunfire announced Camilla's reinforcements converging on their position. Jordan returned fire until he was forced to reload again.

"This is my last magazine," he whispered to Sadler. "I need to find that remote detonator and blow the towers."

Jordan handed Sadler his rifle and drew one of his two handguns. "Cover me and then try to make it to that door." Jordan pointed to the one door that led back down into the hotel, several meters away. "I won't blow the towers until we're close enough to duck inside."

Sadler nodded.

Jordan sprang out from behind the AC unit and shot a soldier who was closing on their position. Jordan's bullet caught him in the back of the neck, between flak jacket and helmet. He dropped in a spray of blood. Another soldier ahead of him took aim but fell from a burst of gunfire from Sadler. Jordan didn't look back to thank him but ran as fast as he could in the direction he'd seen the remote detonator fall.

Sadler cried out from behind, and Jordan glanced over his shoulder. The big man stumbled backward, out from behind the cover of the massive AC unit. Camilla followed him, kicking and swinging her fists in a fury so fast it was a blur. She had abandoned her pistols in favor of knives; one clenched in each of her hands. Sadler received a couple superficial cuts on his forearms as he shielded his chest from her swings but managed to strike the woman on the side of the head with his large right hand. This dazed her, and he followed up with a kick to her chest that knocked her on her back.

Jordan resisted the impulse to turn back, especially when more gunfire ricocheted off the ground near his feet. He redoubled his run and leapt down to a lower level of the roof. The distance was a little greater than he'd anticipated, and he hit hard, rolled, and came up limping. Though slower now, he did the best he could and started searching for the remote detonator.

After about two minutes he hadn't found the detonator, but he did find Kyle's bag, complete with Molotov cocktails and lighter. He limped toward it, but a flash of light blinded him accompanied by a sharp pain in the back of his head. Jordan stumbled forward and was struck again, this time in the back. He turned just in time to see one of Samson's soldiers raising his rifle and leveling the barrel at his face.

The shot came, not from in front of him, but from behind.

The soldier dropped his rifle and fell to his knees clutching his throat while blood bubbled out of his mouth. Jordan looked up at the level above him, expecting to find Kyle. But it wasn't Kyle.

It was a woman with raven-colored hair and immaculate makeup. She wasn't dressed in her usual pant suit, but instead wore jeans, a tank top, and a thin, leather jacket with her hair pulled back in a ponytail. She lowered her Glock.

"Where's your skull mask?" Agent Kelly asked, sounding a little disappointed.

"I'm not Thanatos," Jordan answered.

He hadn't meant it as a denial of his actions, but as a renunciation of his vigilante persona. He wasn't anything like that monster. He was the one who had stopped The Mad Reaper as a ten-year-old captive. Not even cops or FBI agents had been able to do what he had done. That didn't take away Jordan's guilt, but it did heal something inside his soul and made him want to keep fighting.

"The hell you aren't," Kelly snapped. "I've been following you for days. I know what you've been up to."

The red sedan. Agent Kelly drives a red sedan.

Jordan opened his mouth to answer, but nearly fell over as a wave of dizziness hit. Kelly tucked her weapon into the back of her jeans and scaled a metal ladder down to Jordan's level. Before he knew it she was under his arm, helping him walk.

"I think that asshole cracked your skull," Kelly said.

"Grab that bag." Jordan pointed.

"Why?"

"We need it to escape," he said.

She complied, slinging the bag over her shoulder, then helped him up the ladder. Back up on the upper level, they drew more fire. Jordan returned fire with his handgun, though blurred vision made his aim awful, and he hit nothing. Agent Kelly managed to take out another one of Samson's soldiers and provide cover for them while they crossed open space toward the door that led back into the hotel.

"Wait, there are others with me," Jordan said.

"Shit!" Kelly stopped, and they hid behind a metal casing housing three fans.

Jordan scanned the roof and found Sadler working to fend off Camilla. The big man's suitcoat was tattered and sliced, and his white undershirt was red from blood. He was slowing, and Camilla just kept coming at him.

Jordan pointed at Sadler and Camilla. "He's with me. And she's going to kill him."

"Dammit! Okay, you stay here." Kelly reloaded her gun and bent low, ready to run out from their cover.

"No, I'm coming with you."

"Don't be an idiot! You can barely walk without falling over!"

Before Jordan could argue further, another voice rang out.

"Hey, Puta!"

It was Kyle, standing on top of the tallest water tower.

Camilla stopped her advance on Sadler and looked up at him.

"I'm going to hell now." He held up the detonator. "Care to join me?"

"Oh shit!" Jordan grabbed Kelly's hand. "Find something to hold onto!"

She chose him. She turned and wrapped her arms around him, threading them through the armholes of his flak jacket.

Camilla's eyes widened and she began to run away from Sadler. She'd taken three steps when a thunderous boom and a violent vibration thrummed through Jordan's entire being, and the whole world erupted in light, heat, fire, and water.

The torrent hit Jordan like a truck, and both he and Agent Kelly were swept off their feet and carried like babies toward the edge of the roof. Dazed though he was and afflicted with a double vision that just wouldn't go away, Jordan's adrenaline kicked in, and he grabbed hold of one of the roof's relief pipes. He heaved himself and Agent Kelly up so her back and his midsection lay horizontal across the pipe.

She stared him in the face, her eyes wide, strands of wet raven hair sticking to her forehead. They didn't speak, just held on, staring at each other until the torrent subsided and Jordan was able to relax.

His head throbbed, and he was having trouble focusing. Agent Kelly buried her head in his chest for a moment before extricating her arms from his flak jacket and standing up. She helped him stand.

Jordan surveyed the roof. There were pools and puddles of water everywhere, but no sign of Sadler, Kyle, Camilla, or any of Samson's soldiers. Jordan looked up to where the water towers had been. Each was completely gone, leaving behind only some of the stilts upon which they had sat. Kyle had blown himself to hell. That had likely been his motive for coming on this mission in the first place—suicide. Kevin had suspected it, and Jordan was supposed to have prevented it.

I'm sorry Kevin. I failed you.

Agent Kelly dipped down and came up under Jordan's arm. "Come on."

The bag on her back smelled of accelerant, but the tinkling sound of bottles when she moved told Jordan they still hand some Molotov cocktails left, even if some of them had broken.

And they still had a job to do.

When they made it back down into the hotel, Jordan stopped Agent Kelly on the twenty-ninth floor. "Give me that bag."

"What are you doing?" she protested. "We have to get out of here before more of Samson's men come!"

"We came to save the girls." Jordan growled. "And by God, I'm not leaving until I do!"

The waterlogged woman stared at him and nodded. "Okay, what's the play?"

Perhaps it was the head injury, but Jordan felt a sudden affinity for his new partner. She seemed to understand what was important and wasn't afraid to take the risks required to accomplish it.

"In the bag," Jordan said.

Kelly took it off her back and set it on the ground. She unzipped it and dug inside. Her head snapped up and she narrowed her eyes at Jordan as she pulled a Molotov cocktail out of the bag. "Are you serious?"

"We took the water towers down so the fire suppression system wouldn't put out the flames. That way, when I pull the fire alarm they won't be able to shut it down, and emergency services, and hopefully the press, will have to show up."

"People could get hurt!" She snapped.

"People are already getting hurt!" Jordan grabbed the bottle from her. "At least this way the girls being trafficked here will have a chance to escape."

Kelly looked down at the bag. "What the hell." She shrugged and smiled at Jordan. "Let's burn this bitch down."

Jordan smiled back. After propping the door open, the two moved out of the stairwell and back into what was now the empty orgy room. Using one of the lighters stowed in the bag, Jordan ignited the shredded towel and tossed his bottle. It spun end-over-end and landed on the floor in a pool of liquid fire. Kelly threw her bottle with more power so it broke against the wall. Flames raced up, climbing to the ceiling. They repeated this a few more times until flames spread across the vast room, and the smoke began to choke them both.

"I think it's time to go," Kelly said with a cough.

Jordan nodded, and the two of them made their way back into the stairwell where Jordan located the small red box fixed on the wall. He pulled the fire alarm, causing an earsplitting siren to shriek, magnifying the splitting pain in his head a hundred-fold.

Kelly ducked under his arm again, and they moved as fast as they could down the stairs. It wasn't long before others joined them in the stairwell, flooding in from other floors. The men were mostly middle-aged or older, many wearing only their underwear or slacks and no shirts. The women were, of course, younger, and clad in robes if they were lucky, but most were in lingerie if they had clothes on at all.

A girl cried out above him, and Jordan looked up to see a fat man shoving people aside as he made a mad dash down the stairs. When he neared Jordan, he clotheslined the bastard in his lower jaw. It was meant for his throat, but that was obscured by the man's many chins. The blubbery low life released a very feminine sounding squeal as he went down, becoming the object of scorn and abuse from those who passed by him, many of whom paused to spit on and kick him.

"Feel better?" Kelly asked.

"No." Nausea coursed through Jordan. Not a good sign for a head injury.

They descended several more floors, becoming a veritable parade of fifty or more people, moving steadily. Smoke was starting to fill the stair-well, and Jordan worried that the fire might be progressing faster than he'd anticipated. On top of that, darkness encroached on the edges of his vision, and he had to work to keep it from swallowing him.

"Stay with me, Griffin," Kelly said from far away.

"I'm sorry, Kevin," Jordan said aloud.

"Is that your priest?" She asked. He didn't think she was really asking right now, just trying to keep him talking to keep him conscious.

"He's a good man. He didn't want to do this. I coerced him," Jordan said. If he was going to prison, he wouldn't drag Kevin there with him.

"We're at the fifth floor," Kelly soothed. "We're almost there. Help is coming, okay?"

When had she called for backup? He must be really out of it.

Screams.

A flurry of red.

Kelly shouting.

Pain in his lower back, and motion.

Jordan fell face down on carpet. He raised up on his hands and found himself in a narrow hall running between mostly open hotel room doors.

"You self-righteous zealot!" A woman's voice shouted.

Camilla.

She kicked him in the ribs.

Jordan fell back to the carpet, struggling to breathe.

"Do you know how much Samson's business brings in? AND YOU BURNED IT DOWN!"

A heel landed on his spine. Jordan cried out, and the world threat-ened to vanish into blackness.

Where was Sadler? Had she killed him? Did he get swept off the roof?

The overhead fixtures flickered and winked out, leaving the hall dark save for the dim glow of an exit sign and some lighting along the baseboards.

Camilla knelt in front of him. Her hair was wet and stringy, her nose was bloody, and a large gash marred her otherwise perfect face. She pressed the flat of a small knife against his face.

"You call yourself Thanatos? The god of death?" Camilla barked a scornful laugh at him. "You're not death. You're just a sad, desperate man."

"Who are you?" Jordan managed.

Camilla smiled. "I'm one of the Daughters of Blood. And very soon we'll own this city."

The Mad Reaper, Edward Alexander, the Daughters of Blood. What did it matter which evil he fought? There would always be something else to take its place. It was pointless. It was all so pointless. The darkness waiting at the edges of Jordan's vision grew. He would pass out and Camilla would slit his throat. It was over. The fight was over. Perhaps it had been over the moment he was taken by Thanatos as a child.

It was all meaningless.

No, a voice whispered. And it didn't sound like his voice, but Kevin's. *God chose you to be the one The Mad Reaper kidnapped for a reason. And now you know that reason.*

Those words, spoken from somewhere outside Jordan's mind, but miraculously placed there, were true. He felt their validity like threads of gold spun into his very being. God *had* chosen Jordan to be the one Thanatos stole from his family. And less than an hour ago he'd remembered something long forgotten, long buried. Jordan, as ten-year-old Yuri Ivanov, had killed The Mad Reaper and brought an end to the monster's campaign of horror. There was meaning in tragedy. There was light in the darkness. There was hope. There was a reason to keep fighting.

The darkness trying to swallow Jordan's vision retreated, and for the first time since being struck in the back of the head, he could see clearly.

He locked eyes with Camilla as she smirked at him. "I want to tell you something before I kill you."

She put her lips so close to his ear that they brushed his skin as she moved them. It would've been sensual but for the words that followed, "Your priest, Father Drakes... He's dead. I shot him in the heart."

Kevin was dead. Camilla had killed him. A fire burst to life in Jordan's chest and shot through his extremities. It burned away fear, fatigue, and pain until all that was left was white hot fury.

"Well? Don't you have anything to say?" Camilla asked, her mouth still pressed against his ear.

"Yeah," Jordan said in a low, dangerous voice. "You shouldn't have told me that."

In one explosive motion Jordan grabbed Camilla around the back of the neck, stood, and launched them both to the side, slamming her against the wall.

He adjusted so his right forearm pressed in against Camilla's throat and his left hand held her arm against the wall. She shrieked once, then no more sound came as the pressure of his arm strangled her. Jordan stared into her eyes as they bulged.

"You killed a good man, one who was my friend," he said in that same steady tone. No screaming, no yelling, just a judge stating the charges and then the sentence. "I'm going to kill you."

The look on Camilla's face was one of panic and terror, but that didn't stop Jordan. He just pressed harder. Angry man though he was, Jordan had only known this ultimate state of fury once before—when he killed The Mad Reaper. Kevin would disapprove. This wasn't killing to save life. This was vengeance.

Something sharp dug into Jordan's side. He gasped and released Camilla. She brought up a small knife with her free hand and swiped at his face, but he shoved her, and she stumbled.

"Griffin!" Agent Kelly called from the stairwell door.

Jordan turned to find her silhouetted against the glow of the stairwell's emergency lighting. From what he could tell, she was cradling her right arm. Camilla sprang at him, and Jordan brought up his arms just in time to shield his chest from her small blade, but it caught him across the forearm, biting deep.

Before he could strike back, Camilla pivoted and exploded into a sprint away from him, disappearing into the darkness of the hallway. All of Jordan's weakness returned, and he swayed on his feet, but Kelly was there to catch him before he fell.

"She killed him," was all Jordan could say.

"We can't chase after her. We have to get out before the whole building comes down."

They moved back into the stairwell somewhat slower than before. Kelly was nursing her right arm, and blood ran out from under her sleeve. Jordan tried to look for a tear in her jacket, but he was having trouble seeing again, and blood from a wound in his own side was oozing into his pants.

They finally made it down to the first-floor lobby, which was flooded with dozens of people interspersed with emergency responders of all kinds. Kelly flashed her credentials and kept repeating to any and all that the women here were captives, and the men were to be detained.

The last thing Jordan remembered was the screams as the building shook, then a loud noise and lots of dust.

FIVE ALARM BLAZE BURNS THROUGH DOWNTOWN HOTEL, REVEALS SEX TRAFFICKING RING.

Friday night the exclusive Red Line hotel on Vanderbelt and Cherry caught fire. An apparent failure of the building's fire suppression system allowed the blaze to spread down from the top floors and consume nearly half the building, causing a partial collapse that saw several upper floors fall into the hotel's lobby. The most astonishing twist to this story? The fire exposed the Red Line's horrifying secret; the hotel was a high-priced brothel specializing in serving up captive women, many of whom were underage girls, to rich and high-profile clients. Over two hundred girls were rescued when first responders arrived to combat the blaze, and several prominent men, including an FBI Agent, a judge, and a state senator, were arrested...

ALEJANDRA MORGAN, THE LAKE SIDE GAZETTE

CHAPTER
EIGHTEEN

VICTOR AWOKE to his phone alerting. He'd fallen asleep on the couch, fully clothed. His tongue tasted bitter for some reason, and he glanced at the empty teacup sitting on the coffee table in front of him.

Camilla's tea.

She'd made it for him again to help him sleep through the pain of his bruised and broken ribs. It had tasted stronger than last time and had a strange aftertaste it didn't have before. His head ached, and his thoughts were sluggish.

He groaned as he sat up and reached for his phone. "Yeah?"

No answer came.

Victor looked at the phone and realized he hadn't received a call. He glanced around the room. The digital panel mounted on the wall near the penthouse elevator was the device sounding the alert. Victor gave it a voice command, and a figure appeared on the small panel's display.

"David?"

His friend was soaked from head to toe, cradling his shoulder, his suit jacket tattered and torn, and he was bleeding.

"Victor, please let me up," David begged in a frighteningly weak voice.

Victor fought through the fog of whatever was clouding his mind, ignored the pain of broken ribs, lurched to the elevator doors, and granted access. A moment later the silver doors opened and David spilled out, nearly falling to the ground. Victor caught him before he hit the floor.

"David! Who did this to you?" Victor angrily demanded.

"Camilla."

"What?"

"She's one of the Daughters of Blood, Victor. She wants to take Alexander's place. She's been using us to take over the Underground Empire."

Victor shook his head. "No."

"I heard it from her own lips."

Uncle Simon's laugh roared back to life so loud it forced Victor to squint. He shook his head more vigorously. "No! She wouldn't! She loves me!"

David didn't respond.

Victor looked down at his friend, his brother in all but blood. He'd fallen unconscious. Victor called on the panel next to the elevator again, and the voice of his personal concierge answered.

"Yes, Mr. Reese? How can I help you?"

"I need an emergency transport to my personal surgical team. Tell them to prep for surgery! Mr. Sadler is seriously wounded! I want a team up here with a stretcher, now!"

"Right away, sir!" The concierge answered.

Victor pressed his forehead against David's bloody brow. "You have to hold on."

Something glinted in the light and Victor straightened. A piece of metal was embedded in David's upper chest. It was partially hidden beneath his suit jacket, and Victor moved the cloth aside. A small knife protruded from David's shoulder socket.

Victor ground his teeth as he recognized the rose with a thorny stem engraved on the handle of the knife–it was Camilla's.

I told you so… Uncle Simon said in a sing-song voice.

A plan started to form.

Victor called down to the concierge again and asked that, in addition to the emergency personnel, they send a clean-up crew for David's blood and the water he tracked in.

IT WASN'T long after the cleaning crew left that Camilla returned. In fact, had Victor waited any longer, they might've crossed paths. He'd had time to strip off his shirt and pants—covered in water and David's blood–before she came back, and now he stood staring out over the city with his phone to his ear and his back to the elevator, speaking on the phone to Dawson about the fire at the hotel and what was to come next. He hadn't had to fake that, the calls started coming in soon after David arrived half-dead, first from Alexander himself, informing him of the crisis.

Samson was dead, the Red Line was practically cinders, they'd lost most of their working girls, and several clients were on their way to jail. Clearly David had something to do with that, but his plan, if it worked, would protect David. Victor was somewhat entertained by the fact that Jordan Griffin had been spotted at the Red Line, and it didn't take much to put together why.

"Victor!" Camilla called from behind.

"I'll see you there." Victor ended the call and turned around.

Camilla staggered into the room. She was wearing her red tactical outfit, was soaked from head to toe, and sported several cuts and bruises on her face.

"Where have you been?" Victor rushed over to embrace her. "What happened to you?"

Camilla buried her head in his chest and started sobbing. "David tried to kill me!"

Victor pulled away and stared down at her. "What?"

Camilla nodded. "It's true."

Victor shook his head. "No. He wouldn't do that."

"You think I'm lying?" Camilla pushed Victor away from her. "I told you he hated me!"

Victor ran a hand through his hair. "Why are you dressed in your tactical gear?"

Camilla stared at him for a long moment as if she were considering whether he deserved an answer. She sighed and slouched. "While you were asleep I went to that priest you told me about, the one working with Agent Griffin. I found out David's been working with him too, and they were planning to kill Marshal Samson. So, I followed them to the Red Line to warn Samson. David caught me and tried to kill me, and then he and Agent Griffin burned down the hotel. I think Samson is dead."

"And David?"

Camilla shook her head. "I don't know. Probably dead. *I* barely got away."

Victor embraced her again. "I'm so glad you did. I don't know what I'd do without you."

"What do we do now?" Camilla asked. "David's grudge against Samson has threatened our whole plan, especially if witnesses point the finger at him!"

Victor pulled away and led her to the couch, offering her a glass of bourbon.

"Edward's already called about Samson and the Red Line. I need to go meet with him." Victor hesitated, then said, "I want you to come with me."

Camilla choked on her drink. After she finished coughing, she croaked out, "I shot at him! What if he recognizes me?"

"He won't." Victor motioned at her red outfit. "Unless you wear that." He went into his bedroom and retrieved black slacks and a white button-down shirt before returning to the living room.

Victor stepped into the pants, zipped up the fly, and fastened the button. "We'll claim that you and I have been working together investigating the murder of Escarra. You were, after all, his bodyguard. It'll make sense to Edward." Victor slipped his right arm into the white shirt, wincing as it pulled on his broken ribs.

"And what about your right-hand man working with an FBI agent to kill Samson and burn down the Red Line? How are we going to explain *that*?"

Victor fed his other arm into the shirt sleeve and began buttoning it up. "We're going to blame the murder of Samson and the destruction of his operation on Zhang Min Su as part of her plan to weaken and overthrow Edward."

Camilla was quiet for a moment before nodding in approval and offering, "That could work. But what about everyone who saw David there?"

"I don't know."

Camilla rose. "It's simple. We say he was a traitor working with a crooked FBI agent for Su!"

Victor shook his head. "You know what David meant to me. I won't sully his memory, and if there is a chance he's still alive, we'd be passing a death sentence upon him."

"He tried to kill me, Victor!" Camilla shouted.

Victor stood and turned his back to her.

"You were going to have to make this choice sometime, Victor. Him or me! It's time to choose."

Victor slouched and nodded his head. "I love *you*, Camilla."

Camilla stood and embraced him from behind. "And I love you too. I know this is hard, but betrayals are just steps on the stairs to power."

"I just never thought it'd be him that'd betray me, you know?"

Camilla squeezed him tighter, flaring the pain in his ribs. Victor didn't give her the satisfaction of a pain-response, something he knew aroused her.

"It always hurts worse from those we trust the most," she said.

Uncle Simon giggled.

Victor turned around to face her. "Hurry and go get showered. Edward's expecting us."

She kissed him, then turned and began to disrobe on the way to the shower, glancing back and smirking as her clothes fell to the floor. It made Victor angry that she thought she could control him by means of his libido.

Well, she does have a nice ass, Uncle Simon snarked.

I had some personal suspicions about the way Agent Griffin had been acting, so I followed him to the Red Line. When I realized what was going on there, I confronted Agent Griffin, and he assaulted me, leaving me unconscious in the elevator. The fire alarm woke me up, and when I wandered out of the elevator it was chaos. Fortunately, one of the EMTs found me, and I got out before the ceiling collapsed, thank God.

ASSISTANT SPECIAL AGENT IN CHARGE ADAM
SEIGERS

CHAPTER
NINETEEN

JORDAN WAS at Thanatos's house of horrors again, standing by the dilapidated well. The little blonde girl stood next to him. This time she wasn't a desiccated corpse, but looked like she had on that day he'd approached her in the park–smiling and full of life. Her right hand was in his, her left hand holding a beautiful Barbie doll with a full head of hair and an immaculate, shimmering ballgown.

The little girl looked up at Jordan. "I'm not down there anymore."

Tears poured down Jordan's cheeks, and he knelt to look the girl in her bright blue eyes.

"I am so sorry," he choked out. "Please forgive me."

The little girl smiled and nodded. Then she hugged him and skipped away.

Jordan fell to his knees, bent over, and sobbed.

"It's amazing how easily children forgive," a familiar voice said.

Jordan looked up to see Kevin standing over him, dressed in white and smiling. "I suppose that's why the Lord told us to become as a little child."

Jordan scrambled up and embraced the priest. "Kevin! You're alive!"

Kevin hugged him back, but then pulled away and chuckled. "No, my friend. I'm afraid not."

"Wait." Jordan glanced around. "Am I...?"

Kevin shook his head. "No, you're asleep. Thirty-two minutes post-op to be exact. You had a nasty skull fracture. Your partner saved your life."

Jordan nodded. "Then this is a dream?"

Kevin shrugged. "You'll probably tell yourself that."

"You've come to say goodbye."

Kevin craned his neck to stare up at the sky. "More like, until we meet again."

"Kevin, I need you," Jordan's voice caught. "I don't know what I'm supposed to do now. I think I'm going to prison."

Kevin put his hand on Jordan's shoulder, and it felt warm and as real as when the priest had done it in life. "Your battle isn't finished. There is more to do."

"You spoke to me, didn't you? When Camilla was going to kill me."

Kevin flashed a knowing smile and said, "I told you I was trying to save you, and that hasn't changed. It won't change."

Jordan awoke in a hospital bed surrounded by monitors and tubes. To his relief he wasn't intubated, but his head was wrapped tight, and an I.V. ran from his hand to a bag of fluid that hung over him. His other wrist was handcuffed to the hospital bed rail. He groaned inwardly.

A woman sat in a chair opposite his bed.

"Kate?" Jordan called.

But when his vision resolved, the woman was not his wife, it was

Agent Kelly. She was wearing a blood-stained tank-top and a line of newly sown stitches ran the width of her bicep.

"Your ex?" she said as she set down a book.

"Yeah," Jordan said, trying to hide his embarrassment. "This is her hospital. I thought maybe…"

Kelly glanced at the door. "I'm sorry, she hasn't been in here."

That hit him like a punch to the gut, so he changed the subject before the tears came. Jordan shook the wrist cuffed to the bed rail. "What's this?"

Kelly stood. "Well, you are under arrest."

"For what?"

Kelly scoffed. "Do you really want the list?"

"Constitution says I get one."

"You're the vigilante, Thanatos!"

"Do I look like I'm in any condition to run? Hell, I'm going to have a fight of it just to take a piss."

Kelly stared at him for a long moment before rolling her eyes. "Fine, but I get your story, the full story, you understand?"

Jordan grunted.

Kelly dug out her keys and unlocked and removed the cuffs.

"Who've you told?" Jordan asked.

"Just Morrison."

Jordan nodded. "Can you keep it that way for now? Please?"

Kelly threw up her hands. "I don't owe you anything. You've been a total dick to me."

"I know, and I'm sorry."

She sat back down. "Fine, but now it's time for you to spill your guts. I want to know how you're connected to Thanatos, the real Thanatos!"

Jordan didn't appreciate the demand, so he summed it up as concisely as he could. "When I was ten, he broke into my family's apartment, murdered them, and kidnapped me."

If it shocked Kelly, she didn't show it.

"Wait." She stared at the ground as if she were seeing files in her mind. "There were only a few home-invasion murders attributed to The Mad Reaper, but no kidnappings. One family had a ten-year-old boy.

They were Russian immigrants, the Ivanovs, Serge and Alina. They had a thirteen-year-old daughter, Inessa, and their son was named–"

"Yuri," Jordan finished. "Let me guess, they never found his body."

Kelly's head snapped up and her eyes widened.

"Yeah, that's me."

"What did he do to you?" Agent Kelly asked, but there wasn't pity or even empathy in her question.

Jordan didn't like that, it made him feel less like a person and more like a research project. "He didn't cuddle me and read me bedtime stories, if that's what you mean. But it wasn't what he did to me directly that was the worst thing."

"Tell me."

Jordan didn't answer for a while. Partly because he resented her making him tell his story again, and partly because he was just so damned tired of it all. But finally, when it became clear that the sun would burn out before she would leave his hospital room without the details, he relented.

"He made me lure victims to him, so he could kidnap them. It started with women, then teenage girls, and then, finally, he made me get him a little girl about six-years-old. He forced me to watch him torture and kill her, and then I had to drop her body down a well. After her, he wanted to take another little girl, but I refused to help him. That's when he threatened to torture and kill me."

"What'd you do?" Agent Kelly leaned forward. "How'd you get away?"

"I didn't get away."

Agent Kelly shook her head. "I don't understand."

"I stabbed him dozens of times in the back."

"You what?"

"I killed The Mad Reaper."

Agent Kelly stood. "But you were only ten. How?"

Jordan tried to shrug. He wasn't sure he pulled it off, but he was sure the motion moved his head, making him grimace with the pain.

"Don't know. Call it adrenaline, call it righteous rage, call it a miracle. But I plunged a knife into that bastard's back when he turned away from me, he went down, and I didn't stop stabbing until I knew he wasn't getting back up. I have the scars on my hands to prove it."

Scars from cuts that until recently he hadn't remembered how he'd gotten.

For once Agent Kelly didn't seem to have anything to say.

"After I put him down, I left his secluded house in the woods, found the highway, and walked until my feet bled. I was picked up by Detective Charles Benson. Only one other person besides you knows my real identity. Father Kev..." Jordan choked and couldn't continue.

"Then you know he's dead." Kelly asked. "How?"

"That bitch in red told me she shot him."

And I'm pretty sure I just spoke to his spirit.

Agent Kelly stood and stared out the hospital window. Jordan could see they were several floors up. Silence settled on the room, and he'd settled into something of a mindless haze when she finally spoke.

"I lost my older sister when I was sixteen. She was nineteen and had just left for university, her first time living away from home." Agent Kelly nervously chuckled. "She was so excited, and I was so jealous. Damn, I hated her, and this was just one more reason why. She was always so pretty and popular, and I was the bookworm-tomboy."

If Agent Kelly was the tomboy of the family, Jordan thought, *what did her sister look like?*

"And here she was getting into college on a swimming scholarship of all things! Not enough that she had the perfect body, but she got into school to show it off in a swimsuit! It drove me crazy."

She shook her head. "After she left home I wouldn't speak to her. Not when she called, not when she wrote. It got so bad that my dad had a talk with me. See, Thanksgiving was coming up and Aubrey was coming home, and he told me I'd better drop my attitude so we could have a nice Thanksgiving."

"I'm guessing Aubrey never came home for Thanksgiving," Jordan said.

Kelly shook her head. "The Monday before Thanksgiving she disappeared from campus. The police found her corpse a few weeks later."

"I'm sorry," Jordan said. "I really am."

She turned around. "I joined the Bureau to find answers, but my investigation eventually led nowhere. It's looking like for me there will be no answers. So, I find some relief in finding answers for other people."

"Why are you telling me this?"

"Because you gave me answers to what I thought was an unsolvable case, and in some twisted, messed up way, that brings me comfort. So, thank you, Jordan."

She shocked him by leaning over the bed and brushing her lips against his. It was quick and could have been called chaste, but even so, it sent a shock throughout his entire body, leaving him speechless.

"I'm going to let you get some rest now and go get some of my own. Don't escape, or I'll have to handcuff both your wrists." She winked and flashed a tired smile before leaving the room.

After she was gone, and after Jordan had successfully wrestled his thoughts back from places they shouldn't have gone, he stared out the window. His mind became a sluggish mixture of memories, both old and new, all miserable and bad. His heart ached, and soon the weariness and the painkillers overcame his anxieties, and he drifted off to sleep.

"En secreto tomamos lo que deseamos. Al aire libre disfrutamos del botín de la conquista. No amamos a ningún hombre. En la sangre estamos unidos. Sangre que usamos. Por la sangre vencemos."

Translation:

"In secret we take what we desire. In the open we enjoy the spoils of conquest. We love no man. In blood we are bonded. Blood we wear. By blood we conquer."

CREED OF THE DAUGHTERS OF BLOOD

CHAPTER
TWENTY

VICTOR'S CAR pulled through the gated fence and began the long ascent up the drive that led to a large Victorian-style mansion. It was the personal residence of Zhang Min Su. Camilla sat next to him in the back seat. She kept nervously glancing at the driver and then out the back window at the car following.

Victor placed a hand on her knee and squeezed. "It's okay, sweetheart. Don't be nervous."

She flashed him a smile and wiped a lock of hair out of her eyes. It had grown longer since they first met and made her look even more beautiful.

It's always hard to break the pretty dolls, Uncle Simon said. *You can keep them for a while, but eventually you have to toss them out.*

Victor looked away from Camilla.

The drive up to the mansion took five minutes. When they arrived they were greeted by Alexander's personal bodyguards, who wanded and disarmed them. Victor pulled a duffle bag from his car that security barely searched and then returned to him quickly. They followed the same tack with his jacket and pants, but they all but harassed Camilla. This set her temper off, and she expressed her displeasure loudly with several Spanish curses while being forced to produce guns and knives from more than one intimate place upon her person.

When they were done with the security check, they were escorted into the mansion and directed to a large room arranged for entertaining guests, furnished with two large, plush leather couches and three companion easy chairs. The walls were decked with modern art and a very large screen on the wall set opposite the couch and chairs was sure to make for an exciting home theater experience.

In the center of the room, kneeling on the floor bound and gagged, was Zhang Min Su and her teenage daughter. Sitting in one of the chairs, enjoying a glass of amber liquid, was Edward Alexander.

"Victor!" Alexander took a large drink and stood, placing the empty glass in the chair's built-in cupholder.

Camilla cast a worried look at Victor.

She's wondering why he's in such a good mood. A very clever one, this girl is.

Victor ignored Uncle Simon. "We came as soon as we could."

Alexander waved the comment away. "Don't worry about it. It is the middle of the night, after all."

Camilla jumped as the room's wooden double doors slid shut behind them.

"So, this is Camilla?" Alexander approached them and reached out to gently cup her chin.

"Yes, sir," Victor answered.

Alexander smiled. "You didn't do her justice when you said she was beautiful."

Camilla smiled and broke Alexander's hold on her chin by dipping her head down in a demure–although very practiced–expression of shy embarrassment. "Thank you, Mr. Alexander."

"What's this?" Alexander asked. He gently traced the gash on her forehead with his index finger. "How did you do this?"

"I was at the Red Line tonight. This cut is one of several injuries I sustained fighting David Sadler. He was trying to kill me. I was trying to stop him from killing Marshal Samson."

Alexander backhanded Camilla across the face. She fell onto one of the leather couches, but was back up in a second, fists raised in a fighting stance, a rivulet of blood leaking from her nose.

"I don't abide liars, Camilla. No matter how pretty they are."

"Victor?" Camilla shot him a confused glance.

Victor didn't look at her. He couldn't. As much as he hated her for what she'd done to David and how she'd used and betrayed him, seeing her in this moment filled him with a surprising sense of pity. Why was that?

It's because you're weak, Uncle Simon said.

"Her real name isn't Camilla. It's Adriana Osorio, and she is a member of the Daughters of Blood syndicate out of Columbia."

"Victor?" Camilla shouted, but it wasn't anger in her tone, it was confusion.

"She's the one who killed Escarra. Since then, she's been trying to infiltrate our operation through seducing me while actually working with Zhang Min Su."

The bound and gagged older Asian woman kneeling on the floor shook her head wildly. Victor met her eyes but said nothing.

"Their plan was to distract me by having Adriana start a relationship with me as we investigated Escarra's murder, while at the same time she and Su were taking measures to make you look weak by sabotaging your operations. They did this by killing Escarra, which ruined our deal with his organization. Then they attacked your guests at your annual Art Gala where Adriana herself made an appearance."

Victor unzipped his duffle, drew out Camilla's red tactical outfit, and cast it at her feet. This time he did make eye contact with her, and what he caught from his lover was a wild-eyed mixture of rage and fear.

"Tonight's assassination of Marshal Samson and the burning down of the Red Line hotel was just their latest and largest effort to hurt you. Had it not been for David Sadler's intervention and his warning to me about what Adriana was doing, information he nearly lost his life obtaining, Adriana and Zhang Min Su may have caused even more damage. Certainly, it would've given Su more time to continue building up her paramilitary forces, something she was planning to augment with South American mercenaries supplied by the Daughters of Blood when she moved on you in earnest. Already she'd received token forces from Columbia to help with their operations."

"Those are serious accusations," Alexander said. "What do you have to say for yourself Su?" Alexander leaned down and removed the gag.

"It's not true, Edward. I swear. I would never betray you! I'm loyal!"

Alexander adopted a mock somber expression and nodded. "So you say. But we have evidence."

That was the cue for Dawson to enter the room dragging two bodies, both South American mercenaries Victor himself had hired to stakeout Su's property. Dawson had sunk meat hooks in the chest of one mercenary's corpse and in the eye of the second corpse for ease of dragging them into the room.

"These men look to be of South American extraction, Su," Alexander said.

"I've never seen these men before!" Su cried.

Alexander clucked his tongue. "They were found here, on your estate."

"Please, Edward," Su sobbed. "I didn't do what he's saying."

Alexander drew a black and silver .38 Special from his jacket and aimed it at the head of Su's daughter. "No more games. Tell me the truth, Su, or I will kill your daughter."

The teenage daughter, with tears already streaming down her face, began to sob harder and say something to her mother around the gag.

Uh oh, Uncle Simon said. *Parents don't usually lie when their children's lives are on the line.*

And sometimes they do, Victor responded.

He hadn't planned for this, but seeing that Alexander had brought Su's daughter into the standoff, he also wasn't surprised something like this might happen, and knowing how much Su cared about her daughter…

Zhang Min Su met her daughter's eyes, and something passed between them. She looked up at Alexander. "Yes, Edward. It's all true."

Now sell it, Su.

"Why, Su?" Alexander asked, and he sounded genuinely hurt. "After all I've done for you? You were my favorite. Do you know that? Out of all the sycophants and yes-men that kiss my ass each day, I always knew you'd be straight with me. I trusted you. Why turn on me?"

Su shrugged. "I thought I could do it better."

Perfect.

Alexander nodded to himself, then shot Su in the head.

Her daughter screamed around her gag and fell onto her mother. Unable to use her bound arms, the child nuzzled Su with her head, sobbing and trying to scream. Without so much as looking at the girl, Alexander put two bullets in the back of her head, and the muffled screaming stopped.

Alexander used his free hand to massage his forehead. "Do what you want with the Colombian bitch, Victor."

Victor stepped toward Camilla. She glanced around the room at the several bodyguards, then, apparently realizing she had no chance of fighting her way out, especially in her exhausted and injured state, she lowered her arms.

"So, you chose David?"

"There was never any choice."

"What now?" Camilla asked. "Are you going to kill me, Victor?"

Victor smiled. "Not me."

Dawson stepped up beside him.

Camilla's eyes widened and she started to visibly shake. Victor had told her a little about Dawson's hobbies. To her credit, she stiffened and glared at the unkempt psychopath. "You better not leave him alone with me. I'll break his neck in under thirty-seconds."

"Oh, I know that," Victor said.

He reached into his jacket pocket, uncapped the syringe he'd been keeping there, then quickly pulled it out and stabbed the needle in Camilla's upper arm.

She gasped.

Victor drew it out and she grabbed her arm at the injection site.

"What did…" She stammered. Camilla staggered and fell.

Victor caught her and lowered her to the couch. She fixed him with a terrified, wide-eyed stare.

"It's a little concoction of mine. A fast-acting paralytic that allows for continued consciousness and increased sensitivity to pain."

"My sisters will come," Camilla slurred. "They'll make you pay for this."

"Maybe." Victor leaned in so his lips were next to her ear and whispered, "You know, I really cared for you. If you hadn't tried to kill David I would've let you go, even though you'd been playing me."

Camilla's dark eyes welled up with tears.

Victor stood and turned to Dawson. "She's all yours."

Dawson grinned, and Camilla tried to work her mouth in what Victor guessed was an attempt to scream, but nothing came out. The unkempt, messy-haired man in a trench coat bent down and picked her up, slinging her over his shoulder. Victor made eye contact with her one last time before Dawson slid open the room's double doors and disappeared.

His heart ached at the sight of her frightened face, but the rage he felt at her betrayal was overpowering the grief, so he held on to that. It became his soothing balm.

There might be some hope for you, yet, Uncle Simon said.

Victor ignored him and turned to face Alexander. He was again sitting in the easy chair sipping from his glass of amber liquid. His men were removing the bodies of Su and her teenage daughter.

"You were right, Victor." Alexander sighed. "It seems I can trust no one."

"If I may make so bold, sir. You can trust me."

Alexander looked up at him and smirked. "Said the scorpion to the fox."

"I did just hand my woman over to a murderous, sexual sadist because she betrayed you."

Alexander took another sip. "Was she really your woman though?"

Victor sighed and sat on the arm of the leather couch. "No, I suppose she wasn't."

Alexander narrowed his eyes at him and then arched an eyebrow. "You're genuinely heart broken."

Victor straightened. It was the truth. And Alexander was a keen one for recognizing it. It was a reminder to Victor to tread carefully and not underestimate his enemy.

"I was deceived. If it hadn't been for David..."

Alexander nodded. "Still, in the end you did what had to be done, and you delivered on your promises to me. You have earned trust with me, Victor. But remember, trust is a capital that can be compounded or squandered. Continue to build on this foundation and you will remain in my favor. You know the consequences for acting against my interests, even inadvertently."

"I do sir."

Alexander drained his glass. "Now, tell me. How do you think I should clean up this mess and shore up my reputational strength?"

Victor smiled. "I have some thoughts on that."

Alexander waved. "Let's hear them."

"First, you need to cut up Su's corpse and send a piece of it to each of your remaining underbosses. Seize all her assets and take them for your own, then handpick someone to take over her operation. Execute her lieutenants and her remaining family members and anyone she loved even if they weren't involved in the organization. All this will send a message."

"Ruthless, but not really outside-the-box thinking, Victor."

This is where Victor's plan succeeded or failed. It all led up to this moment. He tried not to show any nerves. "Then give an order that your underbosses are no longer to have any kind of organized armed body of enforcers–no more soldiers. They get a handful of personal bodyguards, and that's it."

Alexander straightened. "Are you *trying* to provoke a revolt?"

Victor put his hands up. "Please, hear me out."

Alexander motioned for him to continue.

"We organize a paramilitary force, highly trained, like you've done with myself and the men under my command, but instead of twenty-five hundred, we grow that number to twenty-five thousand. A small army to keep the other bosses in line. Ostensibly we are there to do their bidding, to act as their enforcers and protect them from one another, but we're really your force to keep them in line and ultimately prevent anymore situations like the one with Su."

Alexander sat in silence for several agonizing minutes before finally asking, "And I suppose *you* would lead this force?"

"It would make the most sense."

Alexander flashed a knowing smile. "Twenty-five thousand would be a small army indeed, a number nearly to rival that of the city's police force. How would you raise such an army?"

Victor smiled. "We start with the Lethal Games, add a number of satellite tournaments, and keep it running nearly twenty-four-seven. These lower tier tournaments don't need to feed into the main event, and we recruit winners from there. We can also send scouts to group meetings for able-bodied veterans struggling with PTSD. Those men are vulnerable and often looking for another cause for which to employ their skills. And speaking of military, we can also place some of our people in Army/Navy recruitment centers. They can send us those who are screened out for psychiatric and criminal history reasons."

"I can see you've thought this through, Victor." Alexander stood. "Let me ask you this, once you command all these men in my name, what's to stop you from overthrowing me?"

"Aside from my demonstrated loyalty, sir?"

Alexander waved at the blood on the carpet. "Su was loyal."

Victor thought for a moment. Honesty was the only way he'd ever made any progress with Alexander. How could he lie using honesty?

And then it hit him.

Oh, you are a clever boy, Uncle Simon laughed. *Your talents are wasted here.*

"Sir, I think you, like me, realize that true power comes not from money or weapons, but from information—or secrets rather. So as collateral against my loyalty, I will give you one of my secrets, a closely guarded one that you can use against me should you suspect me of disloyalty."

Alexander expectantly stared at Victor.

"I have someone I care about very much—a twin sister. I've gone to extraordinary lengths to keep her identity and very existence a secret."

"Yes, you have." Alexander cocked his head, studying Victor. "I make it a point of pride to know everything about those who work for me, especially the ones I keep close, and I never knew this."

"I will give you her information, and you can keep her under watch with orders to kill her if I ever so much as telegraph a move against you. Does that reassure you?"

Alexander grinned.

Special Agent in Charge Thomas Morrison, Inside, along with my confession, you'll find a journal detailing my interactions with one of your agents, Jordan Griffin. This is for your eyes only, and I am not submitting it as evidence...

LETTER FROM FATHER KEVIN ALLEN DRAKES

CHAPTER
TWENTY-ONE

JORDAN SAT at the table in the conference room of his FBI field office. Gone was his dirty blond hair, shorn for surgery, replaced with tightly wrapped bandages. A pair of crutches leaned against the glass table next to him. Along with his skull fracture, he'd managed to badly sprain his ankle and take a knife wound to his left side. Fortunately, the knife wound was superficial, as were the rest of his injuries.

Next to him sat Agent Danielle Kelly, dressed in another pressed and pristine pant suit with hair, nails, and makeup appearing to be done by professionals, though Jordan knew better. She caught him looking at her and winked. Jordan blushed and looked away. He was still trying to decide if she was interested in him or just a playful flirt. Either way it made him uncomfortable, though not as uncomfortable as before today—he having received notice via email a few hours prior that his divorce was now final.

He'd tried to call Kate several times while in the hospital, but she wouldn't answer. And despite his hopes and prayers, she'd not come to see him. He'd gone looking for her, which had upset some of the nurses and forced them to reveal that Kate had taken a leave of absence the moment she'd found out Jordan had been admitted. That almost hurt worse than if she'd just been avoiding coming to his hospital room.

It was probably for the best. Although not yet arrested, Jordan was headed to prison, and Kate didn't need that. That's what this meeting was sure to be about, his official dismissal pending an investigation, or perhaps, if things were moving quicker than that, his arrest and being remanded to the Lake Side police.

For the briefest of moments he'd thought about trying to run, but that wasn't who he was, and he could hardly walk, let alone run. He glanced at the crutches and chuckled to himself. That was a surprise. When was the last time he'd genuinely laughed?

He'd been different since the hotel. Different since he'd recovered his memory of killing Thanatos—more solid, more himself, more whole. He wasn't healthy yet, not by a hundred miles, but he'd made progress. Sad that'd it'd taken such extremes to put him on that path. Would prison derail him? Throw him back into the abyss of self-loathing and mental descent?

Your battle isn't finished. There is more to do, Kevin's voice whispered from his memory.

The conference room doors opened, and Morrison entered, carrying a brief case followed by ASAC Adam Seigers.

Seigers, wearing a neck brace and sporting two black eyes and a splint on his nose, motioned at Jordan. "What's this piece of shit doing here? Why isn't he in cage downtown?"

Jordan growled and moved to rise when a soft hand covered his clenched fist. He glanced to his right to find Kelly looking at him. She shook her head slightly and mouthed "Wait."

Jordan forced himself to relax and sit back.

"A little professionalism, please, Seigers?" Morrison chided.

The injured ASAC glared at Jordan and moved to sit at the head of the table next to Morrison where he continued to stare at Jordan. He met Seiger's stare with one of his own until Agent Kelly slapped his leg under the table.

He looked at her, and she whispered, "Stop the dick measuring."

Jordan sheepishly nodded and focused on the notepad in front of him.

"Agent Griffin," Morrison began, "I've called this meeting to address some very serious accusations that have been made against you."

"Tom, if you'll just give me a chance to explain—"

"I didn't say you could speak, Agent Griffin!" Morrison snapped.

Jordan fell silent. He caught a smug smile on Seiger's face.

Morrison deeply inhaled and drew three forms from his briefcase. "But first, I have three signed affidavits here from underage girls rescued from the Red Line that can positively identify Special Agent Seigers as having availed himself of their services on several occasions." Morrison swiveled in his chair to face his assistant. "We even got a rape kit from one of the girls who you paid for the night the hotel was destroyed."

Seigers turned pale. He sputtered and shook his head. "Tom, what is this? What are you—"

"- Shut up, Adam!" Morrison stood and leaned down to stare Seigers in the face. "Here's what's going to happen. I'm going to fire you for sexually harassing Agent Kelly over there."

"It's true," Agent Kelly said. "He grabbed my right buttocks on his way into the room."

Seigers, eyes wide and mouth agape, glanced at Kelly then back at Morrison. "But my pension..."

Morrison grabbed Seigers by the front of his shirt. "Oh, you have a lot more to worry about than losing your pension, friend. Do you know what they do to feds in prison? Or to feds who like to diddle little girls?"

Seigers worked his mouth like a fish, but nothing came out.

Morrison continued in a low, dangerous tone that Jordan had never heard from him in all the years he'd known the man. "I'm going to fire you, and you're going to forget you ever saw Agent Griffin at the Red

Line. If anyone asks about it, because I know you've run your mouth, you're going to tell them it was a lie to try and save yourself from getting fired. If you don't agree to my terms, I will have you arrested, prosecuted, and you will go to prison where your asshole will expand and your lifespan will shrink. Do you understand me?"

Seigers nodded.

Morrison let go of him. "Your credentials and your weapon on the table now."

Seigers dropped his badge and gun on the table.

"Now get the hell out of here." Morrison pointed. "Don't clean out your office, just go and never come back."

Seigers rose and rushed out of the conference room without so much as glancing at Jordan or Kelly.

Jordan looked at Morrison, opened his mouth, but didn't know what to say. Finally, he found the words. "Tom, you could lose your career for that. I don't know how to thank you."

Morrison, who was staring at the affidavits on the table, looked up and locked eyes with Jordan. "My job is to get justice for the victims of horrendous crimes and to make the perpetrators of those crimes pay. I just let a monster walk free to ensure you don't go to prison, and in the process, denied these three girls their justice, so don't thank me!"

Jordan didn't know how to respond to that so he didn't say anything.

Morrison sat down in his chair and pulled other items from his briefcase: two envelopes, one opened and one not, and a small leatherbound journal. "The open letter was from Father Drakes to me. He explained what you two have been up to but took full responsibility for it. He said he used his education in psychology to manipulate you into committing vigilante assaults. He asked that I do all in my power to work with the courts to see that you are shown leniency and receive psychiatric help instead of jail time in exchange for his confession and guilty plea."

Jordan's eyes burned and hot tears spilled out. "He was going to go to prison for me?"

Morrison nodded. "The journal details what was really happening, including some interesting information about your connection to The Mad Reaper, something Agent Kelly has corroborated and expanded upon."

Jordan wiped his eyes and shot a glance at Kelly.

She shrugged. "You never said I couldn't tell anyone."

Morrison continued. "Father Drakes asked me to keep the journal a secret. Apparently, he wanted someone to know what really happened and said from what he learned about me through you, he felt like he could trust me with it. He also said with him in prison, you would need someone to help you find your way back."

"And the third letter?" Jordan asked with a sniffle.

"That's from Father Drakes to you." Morrison tossed it to him. "Read it later."

Jordan nodded. "So, what now? Kevin's dead. Are you just going to cover up what I've done?"

Morrison turned his chair and stared out the window at the skyline of Lake Side City. "Federal Judge Evan Devereux, U.S. Congressman Glen Wainwright, and business mogul Blake Singh were arrested at the Red Line. All three have been released with charges dropped."

"What?!" Kelly shouted.

Jordan slammed his fist down on the glass table, leaving a crack in the glass.

Morrison continued, "We have no proof, but it's clearly Alexander's doing."

"How are we supposed to fight him when he's tainted the whole system?" Jordan balled his fist where it had impacted the glass. He stared at it as a trickle of blood oozed out from underneath it.

Morrison touched Kevin's journal. "The same way you and Father Drakes did." He swiveled to face them. "By going outside the system. By fighting fire with fire."

Jordan snapped his head up.

Your battle isn't finished. There is more to do.

"So, to answer your question, no, what I did with Seigers wasn't to cover for you, Jordan. I need your help." Morrison looked at Kelly. "Now's your chance to get out of this. If we get caught it'll mean our careers and almost certainly prison."

She glanced at Jordan then back at Morrison and smiled. "It *was* kinda fun burning down that hotel."

Morrison smiled a sad smile. "I hate that it's come to this, but we've tried to fight Alexander's organization the proper way. When the rules of the game make it impossible to win, it's time to cheat."

"So how does this work? I had Kevin. He fed me information. We don't have an informant anymore." *Could they turn David Sadler?* Jordan didn't think so, not if it hurt Reese. For some reason Sadler was loyal to the man. That was if Sadler was even still alive.

Morrison sighed. "We're going to have to start small and move very carefully. Recruitment will be slow, but I believe we can build a network of informants and powerful people in authority who are just as frustrated with the corruption in the system as we are and who are willing to take drastic, extra-legal measures to bring down Alexander's syndicate. And that will be our singular goal–taking down his Underground Empire. When that's accomplished, we will disband. If we don't have a sunset clause built into our charter, we risk replacing Alexander when we defeat him."

Kelly laughed. "A righteous mafia. I like it."

"It could work," Jordan said.

"We'd need a name, or something we could recognize each other by, like a symbol," she said.

"Before I left to attack the Red Line, Kevin gave me a blessing in Latin." Jordan's voice caught, and it took a beat for him to compose himself. "I remembered some of the words, and while I was in the hospital, I was able to look it up and figure out it was the blessing of St. Michael. What if we used the symbol for St. Michael. It's a sword or scales or both. Seems appropriate, and it's common enough with Catholics to not draw abnormal attention to us."

Morrison smiled. "I like that. And a name?"

"We can call ourselves The Sword of St. Michael, or just The Sword," Jordan answered.

"A tad dramatic," Kelly said, then she grinned. "But I like it."

The conversation continued for another two hours, the three of them brainstorming all the names of potential recruits into "The Sword." While Kelly and Tom were engaging in a discussion about whether a certain judge could be trusted, Jordan opened the envelope containing the letter Kevin had written him. It read:

Jordan,

I know you're probably angry with me. I also know that it may take a while for you to understand why I've done this. But better for me to go to prison than for you to get yourself killed, or worse, kill yourself. Or worse yet, give into your rage and start murdering people. I know you've killed in war and in the line of duty, and have asked me several times what difference does it make? Well, the difference comes down to what's in your heart. As the Bible teaches us, God looks on the inner man. Killing in defense of life is not the same as killing in a vengeful rage.

Jordan paused. He almost killed Camilla. Had she not stabbed him, he would've choked her to death. How would Kevin have reacted to that?

You are a good man, Jordan. Only the men with potential to be the best of us suffer the most in this life, and I know you've suffered in rare and horrible ways, but you must not let that suffering define you. You are not your pain! It's time to heal and move on. It's time to let go of the guilt. The deal I'm hoping to make with the authorities will require you to get help. I pray you'll embrace that help. I also pray you'll fight for a second chance with your wife. I want only happiness for you. And don't worry about me. Prison can't be all that different from seminary – surrounded by cranky, celibate men who read their Bibles and fight over which bunk is theirs. And if you ever forgive me, maybe stop by and visit once in a while?

There is one more thing I want to tell you. It's about a recurring dream I've had for years. I had it again the night you trashed my file room. I don't know why, but it felt relevant after that night for some reason. It goes like this:

I'm outside my old rectory, gardening. In this garden there are all kinds of flowers from all over the world. I'm tending to some Sweet Williams when I notice an uprooted rosebush cast aside on the garden path. It's small and its red roses are in perfect bloom, but its roots are exposed and it's lying where dozens of people will walk in just a few minutes when the rectory opens. So I stand, and I hurry over to where the rosebush is lying on its side and reach down for it. But for some reason I hesitate. I can't explain it, but the rosebush feels dangerous. I visually inspect it to make sure there isn't a spider or small snake hiding in it, and not finding any hidden dangers, I dismiss the fear and pick it up. Right away one of the thorns pricks my thumb, deep. I drop the rosebush and examine my thumb to find I'm bleeding, and not just a little–I'm hemorrhaging. I try to walk to find help, but I become lightheaded and fall to the ground. After that I wake up.

I'm not sure what the dream means, but I feel it is prophetic—not that I'm a prophet. But in Acts it does say God will pour out His spirit in the last days and men will dream dreams. I feel this is like that. I share this with you because I believe it somehow has to do with my fate and this path we've taken. We'll see, I guess.

Camilla was the rose bush, of that Jordan had no doubt. He gripped the letter tighter.

It's time to stop living in the past, Jordan. The peace you seek lies ahead not behind you. God loves you and so do I. Your friend, Kevin Drakes.

P.S. - I know I have no right to ask this, but please consider this request. Will you please befriend Kyle Carter. With me going away, he's going to need a friend. As I've said before, you two have a lot in common—generally speaking, of course. I worry he's not as strong as you, and I think you could really help him.

Jordan wiped a tear from his eye, folded the letter, and put it back in the envelope. He couldn't help Kyle now, but Jordan *would* seek that road to peace. For himself and for Kevin, but first, he had to take a detour. First, he had to bring down Edward Alexander.

EPILOGUE

KYLE CARTER

KYLE STUMBLED down the alleyway toward the warehouse. Being drunk blurred his vision and made walking in a straight line difficult, but apparently it also had its advantages—like making one's body loose enough to survive a three-story fall onto a balcony with little more than bruising. Father Drakes would've called it divine intervention.

Kyle called it bad luck.

He'd scared the hell out of the poor working girl who'd been preening herself in the mirror when he'd splashed down just outside her room. She'd let him in, sopping wet and bleeding. It took him forever to convince her she needed to get out of the hotel. The fire alarm sounding helped.

Sadly, her handlers hadn't wanted her to leave, forcing Kyle to convince them with his fists and feet that the girl could do what she wanted. After he'd put down the men, the girl wouldn't leave, and it became Kyle's job to escort her out of the building, which it turned out was more than on fire, it was burning down.

His suicide attempt having failed, Kyle made sure the girl was safe, and then he slipped off into the night. The next night he'd stopped by church to confess his sin to Father Drakes, but the priest wasn't there. And he wasn't there the next night, or the next. Finally, Kyle asked one of the other priests, and that's when he learned Father Drakes was dead–killed the same night he'd teamed up with Sadler and Agent Griffin. If that wasn't a flashing, neon sign that it was time to die, he didn't know what was.

Kyle walked up to a man in a silver suit standing outside an open rolling door. Kyle handed the man a wad of cash–the entry fee. The man quickly counted the wrinkled bills.

"Shiiit, this's barely a hundred."

"It's all I got," Kyle slurred.

"And are you drunk?" The man in the silver suit waved the hand holding Kyle's cash. "Get lost!"

Kyle shrugged and reached for the money, but Silver Suit drew back his hand. "This is for wasting my time."

Kyle took a step toward Silver Suit who responded by quickly drawing a gun from his waistband and aiming it at Kyle's head.

"I-said-get-lost!"

Kyle stared him in the eyes. "Fine." He started to turn away, but it was a feint that he suddenly turned into a whirl. He spun, stepped inside Silver Suit's defenses, and brought his elbow down onto his extended gun arm. The gun barked out a shot followed by the sound of shattering glass.

The guy cried out, dropped the gun, and cradled his broken arm. "Son of a bitch! You broke my–"

Kyle snapped a jab into the bridge of the man's nose, and he dropped. Then he bent over him and retrieved his crumpled cash. He started as laughter erupted from three other men dressed in similarly expensive suits watching from inside the building. Kyle imitated an elegant bow but stumbled at the last moment eliciting another wave of laughter. He turned and weaved back down the alley. He was going to have to find another way to end his life today.

"Wait!" someone called.

Kyle tensed. Was he going to have to fight all of them? He turned to see one of the men in suits approaching him. This one was tall, with wavy black hair, and was set apart from his companions by the absence of a tie. He stopped just outside Kyle's reach.

He's smart. Maybe one of the champions here?

The man removed his sunglasses. "What was that all about?"

Kyle pocketed his cash. "Your man said I didn't have enough to buy into the games but wouldn't return my money."

The man chuckled, then stepped closer. He slowly reached for the chain around Kyle's neck, pulled out his dog-tags, and read the embossed letters and numbers. "Corporal Carter?"

Kyle swiped the tags out of the man's hand, spun, and walked away.

"I'll pay your entrance fee," the man called.

Kyle stopped and turned. "Why the hell would you do that?"

The man smiled. "I'd love to watch a Navy Seal tear his way through the usual thugs we get here."

"I'm not a Navy Seal anymore."

The man shrugged. "You've clearly retained the training."

"You the boss here?"

The man smirked. "I'm Victor."

"One of the champions then?" The man, Victor, had the confidence and poise of someone who knew how to fight. He didn't show it off like others did, and that meant he was smart, which also meant he was dangerous.

"I was, years ago."

Kyle nodded. "Okay, I'll fight if you pay."

"Great!" Victor motioned for Kyle to follow him, and the two entered the building.

Once the entrance fee was paid, Kyle was handed off to one of Victor's men who took him to a locker room and provided him with trunks and a mouthguard, which Kyle snickered at since each match was to the death. The least of his worries would be biting his tongue or losing a tooth, but he guessed most contestants thought differently. They'd want to protect their teeth because they planned to live. Not Kyle. He wasn't here to win. He was here to die.

He tossed the mouthguard into an open locker and began to undress. A woman clad in a bikini top, booty shorts, and sporting fishnet stockings walked into the locker room just as Kyle was slipping on his trunks. She looked him up and down and flashed a wicked, ruby-lipped smile.

"Can I help you?" Kyle tried not to show his embarrassment by turning and starting to wrap his hands in white tape.

The woman laughed. "You shy or something?"

"What do you want?" Kyle snapped.

The woman frowned. "I'm here to get your name."

"It's Kyle Carter."

"Not your real name. Your fighter name."

Kyle rolled his eyes. "Do I have to have one?"

"Yeah," the woman answered. "All our contestants have one."

Kyle ground his teeth. Why hadn't he just blown his damn brains out? Why pick this way to die?

Because it's not really suicide this way.

Kyle turned away from his open locker. "K.C."

The woman's smile returned. "I like it."

After dressing, he was escorted into another room with screens and a digital leader board displaying all the ranking fighters, their odds of winning, and the tournament bracket. His first match would be against some asshole calling himself "The Hurricane."

He was starting to sober up, and having vowed not to die sober, Kyle found the girl who'd walked in on him in the locker room. "Shey" she called herself, and although she kept tracing his shirtless muscles with a neon pink claw and making not so subtle insinuations, she wouldn't agree to fetch him a drink. Apparently, that was against the rules. The most he could get was a bottle of water and a protein bar. In his last moments, Corporal Kyle Carter truly was bereft of everything, including his right to die plastered.

When the time for his match came, Kyle strode past the raucous crowd without even acknowledging them. He climbed into the caged arena and moved to his corner to wait for *The Hurricane.* Seconds later a tall, muscled man covered in tattoos showboated as he made his way to the ring. The crowd roared with delight as he cracked his inked neck and threw a few air punches.

I'm too tired for this shit, Kyle thought.

And he was tired. Tired of fighting. Tired of weeping. Tired of drinking. Tired of living.

Hurricane climbed into the ring, the chain-link gate was closed and locked, Kyle met him in the center of the ring, and the announcer proclaimed the beginning of the match. Hurricane grinned, showing off a gold tooth, and then swung for Kyle's head. The punch connected with Kyle's temple, showering his vision with an explosion of stars. He staggered back and shook his head to clear his vision.

Kyle had let Hurricane hit him, and the stars and the double vision were expected. What wasn't expected was the inferno of rage boiling up inside of him. It shocked Kyle. He hadn't felt much since the funeral–just a gray, hollow emptiness. The anger he now felt was like being woken up by a splash of ice water. The fire inside him burned hot and it felt... good.

The Hurricane was laughing and blowing kisses to Shey who was cheering him on just outside the cage. Kyle tightened his wrapped fists, straightened, and stepped toward his opponent. The Hurricane turned to fully face him, laughed, and said something, but Kyle didn't hear it. His roar drowned out Hurricane, the crowd, and the whole world.

Hurricane swung, but Kyle deflected the punch with his off hand and delivered a downward strike. Hurricane staggered back apace, but Kyle didn't let up. He moved in, landing punch after punch.

An image of a small coffin being lowered into the ground formed in Kyle's mind. The image was fuel for his fire. Hurricane was spitting out blood, his face swollen, and his eyes now little more than slits, but Kyle didn't stop. He rushed Hurricane, grabbed him around the waist, and lifted him before bringing him back down and slamming his body onto the mat. Kyle dove down with him, Hurricane's head pinned between Kyle's legs as he pulled on the man's arm. Hurricane's neck snapped with a satisfying *crunch*. The crowd exploded into a deafening chorus of cheering.

Kyle released the man's lifeless body and stood. The officials opened the chain-link gate, climbed in, and took Hurricane's pulse. When it was clear the man was dead, the official signaled the announcer who proclaimed, "K.C. is the winner!"

The rest of the night was a blur of blood and bone-breaking. Match after match, and Kyle wasn't slowing down. He also wasn't dying. The rage inside him seemed to take over with each new opponent, and it was as if Kyle was watching the fights from outside his body.

The final fight of the night ended with Kyle covered in a dozen men's blood mixed with his own. Sweat poured down his head as he stared at the dead man lying on the mat before him. The crowd screamed as the announcer shouted something about having a "new champion of The Lethal Games!"

ABOUT THE AUTHOR

JASON JAMES KING

JASON KING would say he's a lover, not a fighter, but really isn't good at either. He was born and raised in Salt Lake City Utah, shaped by the dark forces of 16-bit consoles, anime, junk food, and tabletop games, and was mentored by the ghost of an Aztec shaman.

Jason is married (sorry ladies) to a wonderful woman and has four incredible children from a previous marriage. He loves to laugh, eat, write, and not always in that order and sometimes simultaneously – though that has led to some near-death choking incidents. He's the author of several fantasy novels, a frequent guest at comic and writing conventions, a grateful member of The Church of Jesus Christ of Latter-day Saints and is the President of Immortal Works Press.